I0612100

Queer Bait

Men in Love and Lust #2

Michael Bracken

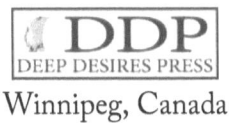

DEEP DESIRES PRESS

Winnipeg, Canada

Copyright © 2023 by Michael Bracken
Introduction © 2023 by Neil S. Plakcy
Front cover design copyright © 2023 Ginny Glass
Cover layout copyright © 2023 by Story Perfect Dreamscape

All characters are age 18 and over.

This is a work of fiction. Names, characters, business, places, events, and incidents are either products of the author's imagination or used in a fictitious manner. Any resemblances to actual persons, living or dead, or actual events is purely coincidental.

No part of this book may be used or reproduced in any manner without written permission from the publisher. However, brief quotations may be reproduced in the context of reviews.

Editor: Francisco Feliciano

Published September 2023 by Deep Desires Press, an imprint of Story Perfect Inc.

Deep Desires Press
PO Box 51053 Tyndall Park
Winnipeg, Manitoba R2X 3B0
Canada

Visit http://www.deepdesirespress.com for more scorching hot erotica and erotic romance.

For Temple
My Love, My Muse, My Everything

CONTENTS

INTRODUCTION
Neil S. Plakcy

A good story is a good story, whether it has erotic content or not. And the pieces included in this collection are good stories.

Of course, I may be prejudiced, because several of them were included in anthologies I edited for Cleis Press. But the experience of putting together those volumes, as well as writing my own gay erotica, has given me a good sense of what makes a story sexy, intriguing, and worth reading.

My first published story, under the pseudonym Dirk Strong, was called "The Cop Who Caught Me" and sold to *Mandate*, a gay magazine that combined sexy picture layouts with erotic fiction. That was over thirty years ago, and writing that story, and many others, gave me the entrée I needed to begin editing those Cleis anthologies.

A good story needs to be well-written. Michael Bracken writes strong, propulsive sentences with great descriptions that bring the reader right into the characters' bedrooms—or wherever else they're getting it on.

Here's an example from "Mutable Memories," the story that kicks off the collection.

"Fairchild had the physique of a man who had never lifted a finger in hard labor. Blue-eyed, sandy haired, clean-shaven, pale of skin, and with little body hair save for the nest cradling his cock and balls, he reminded me of a man much younger than his years. I felt my cock stir at the sight of his nudity just as it had the first time I'd seen him in the bathhouse and nearly every time since."

It not only describes the narrator's boss but give us some insight into how they met. Then compare that to this exchange, which begins "The Gimp, the Vig and The Ring."

> "I lifted Jimmy the Gimp by the lapels of his shirt and pushed him back against the brick wall. "You don't have the money," I said, "you know what I got to do."
>
> "Give me a break," the little guy squealed. "I never been late before."

The description and the language take us right into the story. And then Bracken writes, in "The Gunsel, the Nance, and the Red-Headed Rooster."

"He ankled his way to the Ameche and dropped a dime. When Bertha, the old broad who ran the rooming house, picked up the other end of the line, the gunsel asked two questions. After he heard the answers, he left a half on the counter for the waitress and returned to his flivver. He reloaded his Tommy gun and then drove downtown."

You can't get language more evocative of time and place than that. Another of the delights of this collection is the way it moves so seamlessly from the historical to the contemporary, all the while taking us on an erotic journey rooted in characters so real, they jump off the page.

The descriptions of sex are great, too, as in this example from "The Gimp":

> He grabbed the bath mitt first, lathered it up with lavender-scented antibacterial body wash and began scrubbing my back and my chest. He worked his way down my body until he was kneeling on the tile floor in front of me, the warm water cascading over us from two separate showerheads and my erect cock bobbing in front of his face.
>
> He used the bath mitt to scrub my heavy ball sac as he leaned forward and took the head of my cock into his mouth. He hooked his teeth behind the spongy soft glans and then bathed my cock head with his tongue.

And then there's this passage, from the college-set "What a Rush."

> "My cock stiffened as he massaged my balls, and the towel tented in my lap. Kyle wrapped his fist around my cock and jerked me off, his strokes

hard and fast, and before I could stop myself, I came."

That's important to the reader. We want to feel immersed in stories about real people who have great sex—something we might strive for ourselves, if only we meet the right guy who has the right equipment.

Bracken's characters are so real, like the pickpockets of "The Hitter and the Stall" and the private eye of "Stand by Your Man."

I'm a fan of a well-developed setting, too. Bracken has the ability to bring you almost anywhere in the world, from a college frat house to a New York City subway to a wealthy man's country house. The stories range in time, too, and yet you always know where and when you are.

It's no surprise that Bracken has written and published so many stories in so many venues, and has frequently won awards and been short-listed for others.

One of the things I love about Bracken's stories is the way his language suits the setting. In "Mutable Memories," set in 1900, he writes, "Fairchild brought the foul-smelling [carriage] to a halt at the bottom of the steps and climbed out. He peeled off his cloth peaked cap and driving goggles as he bounded up the steps. When I met him halfway, he shoved them into my hands, peeled off his gloves, and quickly unbuttoned his leather storm coat, adding them to my burden."

The variety of language is one of the delights of the collection and says so much about the characters.

Criminals, college kids, demanding bosses—whatever

your interest, you'll find it within these pages. And I hope you'll enjoy them.

—Neil S. Plakcy
Hollywood, Florida

MUTABLE MEMORIES

At the turn of the century, I worked for Michael Fairchild, a confirmed bachelor living off inherited money. In 1900, the day after Christmas, he sent me from the city by train to open up the Connecticut house, to stock the kitchen and bar, and to prepare for the year-end celebration, when he would host several dozen of his equally spoiled friends in a night of drunken debauchery in order to welcome the Twentieth Century.

The housekeeper—an elderly woman who lived with her groundskeeper husband in a cottage on the eastern edge of the property—helped remove and store the sheets that covered and protected the furniture several months of each year. She also gave the entire house a thorough cleaning in preparation for guests, while her husband tidied up the grounds following a Christmas Day storm that scattered several broken branches across the lawn. The entire estate—a furnished eight-bedroom home, several outbuildings that included a water tower to gravity-feed the indoor plumbing, and the elderly couple who cared for it all—had been inherited from Fairchild's grandfather when the old man died during a visit to a bathhouse in the city.

Much of the hard liquor that would be served during the celebration traveled with me by train, and Fairchild's cook, a stout woman who brooked no dissent, gave me a long list of foodstuffs to acquire locally prior to her arrival the Sunday before the grand affair. As per my instructions, I ensured that all was in order when my employer arrived mid-morning New Year's Eve. I stood waiting on the porch as soon as I heard his horseless carriage sputtering up the long drive.

Fairchild brought the foul-smelling thing to a halt at the bottom of the steps and climbed out. He peeled off his cloth peaked cap and driving goggles as he bounded up the steps. When I met him halfway, he shoved them into my hands, peeled off his gloves, and quickly unbuttoned his leather storm coat, adding them to my burden. "Get my bags and take them to my room, Stevens. I need to bathe and change clothes before the guests arrive."

I had a first name, but Fairchild never used it. I replied, "Yes, sir. Right away, sir."

My employer had disappeared into the house by then and I doubt if he heard my response. I shifted my load of discarded driving clothes and grabbed both the valise and the suit bag from the passenger seat of his horseless carriage. Then I followed him inside, past the grandfather clock in the foyer, and carried everything up the stairs to the master bedroom at the far end of the hall. I then hung his storm coat in the wardrobe along with most of the contents of the suit bag and unpacked the valise before putting its contents in the dresser. When I finished, I returned to the main floor and found the housekeeper in a tizzy, as Fairchild had tracked something greasy across the hardwood floor.

After listening to her laud Fairchild's grandfather for his obsessive fastidiousness, and after assuring her that Fairchild would return to the city by week's end, I went in search of her husband.

In the city, people would gather at City Hall Park that night to hear John Philip Sousa's band perform while they watched the century count down on the big clock, but Fairchild had other plans. He had me hire a quintet of musicians from the city to perform lively dance music, and I sent the groundskeeper to the train station to greet their arrival and transport them back to the house.

Once Fairchild was satisfied with the liquor selection, that the cook had things well under control in the kitchen, and that the musicians would soon arrive, I followed him upstairs. While I drew his bath, he stripped off the clothes he'd worn during his drive from the city and tossed them in a heap for me to care for later.

Though he had yet to go to fat, as he would later in life, Fairchild had the physique of a man who had never lifted a finger in hard labor. Blue-eyed, sandy haired, clean-shaven, pale of skin, and with little body hair save for the nest cradling his cock and balls, he reminded me of a man much younger than his years. I felt my cock stir at the sight of his nudity just as it had the first time I'd seen him in the bathhouse and nearly every time since.

"How do I look, Stevens?"

I wet my lips with the tip of my tongue and replied, "Delicious."

My employer smiled and then stepped into the bath. After I scrubbed his back, I left him to finish bathing alone while I laid out his clothing for the evening: a dark blue lounge coat with matching trousers that were cuffed and creased, a white shirt, a dark tie, and two-toned spectators.

I had been with Fairchild since shortly after his grandfather's death, and I attended to his every need, from delivering his breakfast in bed to organizing the orgiastic parties he hosted. He had no particular skill with numbers, leaving me in charge of all his household accounts. Suffice it to say, with his predilections, Fairchild was unlikely to ever produce an heir, and so, with no incentive to safeguard his grandfather's fortune, he spared no expense in his efforts to impress and outspend the wealthy young malingerers with whom he fraternized.

He walked naked into the master bedroom, a towel in one hand. I took it from him and vigorously dried his back, his buttocks, and the nest of his pubic hair, causing his balls to tighten and his cock to stir.

Fairchild pushed the towel away. "Save it for later," he told me. "Guests should be here any moment."

I helped my employer dress and then followed him downstairs to the living room, where I prepared his first drink of the evening. He'd barely finished it before the first guest arrived, a longtime friend of Fairchild's named Winston Carnegie.

All of Fairchild's guests arrived, just as he had earlier,

in horseless carriages, parking the damnable things willy-nilly on the lawn. This gave the groundskeeper apoplectic fits until I convinced him and his wife to return to their cottage and ignore what was happening at the house, and I spent much of the early evening greeting young men at the front door and attending to their driving clothes. Once I felt certain everyone had arrived, I moved about the house, refreshing drinks, collecting empty plates, and appreciating the youthful exuberance of nearly three-dozen young men who valued hedonism above all else and who financed their excesses with the blood and sweat of previous generations.

With pendent lights ablaze in every room, lighting the house up like a Broadway theatre, I was able to examine each of the guests in turn. The young men were mostly clean-shaven, though a few sported moustaches or sideburns. All had hair cut short in the fashion of the day and were dressed much the same as Fairchild. They were of various heights and weights and body shapes, but all shared the pale skin of carefree men who spent far more time in the dark than in the light.

When these men weren't eating, drinking, smoking, and dancing, they were talking. They debated the issues of the day, and they laughed about Mark Twain's "A Greeting from the 19th Century to the 20th Century," published in the *New York Herald* the previous day, and about the predictions of the future published in the *New York World*'s supplement "New York as It Will Be in 1999," also published that Sunday. Did anyone really believe that the city would someday be filled with elevated sidewalks that connected skyscrapers with flat roofs designed for airship landings?

As midnight approached, the guests began to pair off, disappearing into one of the seven guest bedrooms and returning to the party a bit later with disheveled clothing and satiated grins. After alcohol diminished their inhibitions and lowered the social barrier between the spoiled wealthy and the help who attended to their needs, I was propositioned half a dozen times and repeatedly had my ass pinched and my crotch fondled. I smiled through it all, knowing full well that my reward would come later.

After I replaced Winston Carnegie's drink for the second time, he grabbed my arm and said, "You're a godsend, Stevens. How did Michael ever find you?"

"Fate," I replied without elaboration.

After an anomaly in household accounting that a previous employer attributed to my negligence cost me my position, I had been forced to take part-time employment as a towel boy in the bathhouse where I first encountered Fairchild and his grandfather. Invisible to them, I was able to observe their dynamic each time they visited. The allowance Fairchild's grandfather provided wasn't sufficient to maintain the lifestyle Fairchild desired, and the friction between them led to a fatal confrontation.

"Fate?" Carnegie repeated. "I wish fate had dropped you on my doorstep. I'm stuck with a stuffy old codger who's been with the family since my father was a gleam in his father's eye."

"I'm certain your man is quite proficient at his job, sir."

"Oh, Alistair's good enough, but he isn't you," Carnegie said with a wink. "I could have fun with you."

"You still might," I retorted, returning his wink, because I was at all times courteous and accommodating to my employer's friends.

The musicians kept a watchful eye on the clock, silencing the music for a few minutes shortly before midnight. Fairchild led his guests into the foyer for the countdown to the new century, and everyone let out a cheer when the grandfather clock struck the twelfth chime. Then the band played, and the guests sang "Auld Lang Syne" while I opened several bottles of champagne.

Discretion disappeared once the new century began. Jackets came off, ties were loosened, and before long I found one of the guests giving hand jobs to two other guests in the sitting room. Moments later I found a slender brunet bent over the dining room table while a thick-dicked young blond rogered him in the ass.

Of course, I couldn't help myself. Seeing all the naked male flesh—young and seemingly unaffected by the mass quantities of alcohol consumed throughout the evening—made my cock tent the front of my trousers.

Before she had a chance to witness any of the debauchery, I sent the cook out the back door and across the estate grounds to spend the night with the groundskeeper and the housekeeper. I considered dismissing the band as well but had nowhere to send them at that time of night, and so they continued playing as if nothing unusual was happening around them.

Another trip through the house, switching off some of

the pendant lights as I went, brought me back to the foyer, where I found my employer sitting on the staircase, his trousers around his ankles and his cock in the mouth of an unfamiliar blond. Fairchild held an empty whiskey glass in one hand and had the other hand resting on the back of the fellating young man's bobbing head.

"Stevens!" my employer called when he spotted me watching. He held up the empty glass. "Refill this."

"Yes, sir," I said as I took the glass.

Once his hand was empty, Fairchild pressed it against the back of the blond's head and began bucking his hips up and down, face-fucking the young man.

I'd stepped behind the bar in the living room before my employer came, so I didn't see him ejaculate in the blond's mouth, but I certainly heard him shout the name of a popular deity when he did.

When I returned with Fairchild's whiskey, the blond was nowhere to be seen, nor were my employer's trousers and spectators. Fairchild wore his jacket, shirt, and loosened tie, but nothing below that save for his stockings and garters. His saliva-and-come-covered cock was stuck to his thigh, and he unstuck it before standing. He took the drink from my outstretched hand and asked, "Things are going rather well, don't you think, Stevens?"

"Quite well, Mr. Fairchild."

Two naked young men came running from the library, their erections preceding them, and headed up the stairs. Fairchild's gaze followed them. "I think I ought to find out what that's all about."

"Yes, sir."

After my employer also headed up the stairs, I continued patrolling the house, turning off pendent lights as I went. Once most of the downstairs was dark as the night outside, I led the musicians into the kitchen.

A few minutes later, Carnegie found me standing with the band as they wolfed down leftover food. He placed one hand on my back and leaned close to whisper in my ear. "Everyone else has gone upstairs."

"Yes, sir?"

He whispered, "I still think I can have fun with you, Stevens. You're more of a man than any of the boys here tonight."

I certainly was older than Fairchild or any of his guests. "There's only one way to find out, Mr. Carnegie."

He smiled.

I told the band they could sleep on the living room floor if they wished, and that someone would see them to the train station in the morning.

Carnegie had a half-empty glass of whiskey in one hand. After I dipped a cloth napkin in greasy roast beef drippings, I took his other hand and led him to my room in the servant's quarters accessible only through the kitchen. As I closed the door behind us, Carnegie took the greasy napkin from my hand and placed it and his whiskey glass on the nightstand. Then he undressed. When he had removed his trousers and underthings, my cock, already half-erect from several hours spent watching naked young men in various stages of flagrante delicto, immediately stood at rapt attention.

My employer's guest finished undressing and he

helped me do the same, quickly revealing my turgid erection and the wild nest of dark pubic hair surrounding it.

"You've been serving us all evening, Stevens," Carnegie said as he dropped to his knees in front of me. "It's about time someone served you."

He wrapped his fist around my cock and held the shaft tight as he took the mushroom cap of my cock head into his mouth. He licked all the way around, covering it with his saliva, and then he slowly drew in my entire length. As soon as his warm breath tickled my pubic hair, he drew back, catching his teeth on the swollen glans before doing it again.

I wrapped my hand around the back of Carnegie's head and held it as his face moved up and down the length of my stiff shaft, lubricating my cock with so much saliva that it dampened my pubic hair and dripped from my balls. As he fellated me, he grabbed my wet balls with his free hand and used the tip of his finger to stroke the sensitive spot behind them.

He had teased me long enough. I grasped his head and held it as I thrust the entire length of my cock into his mouth. Then I drew back and did it again, fucking his face hard and fast. Just when I was about to come, he slipped his saliva-slickened finger back just a little bit further and pressed it against the tight pucker of my ass hole, which immediately opened to him.

I came and came hard, firing thick wads of hot come against the back of Carnegie's throat. He swallowed every drop and held my cock in his mouth until it stopped spasming.

He stood, washed down my load with the last of his whiskey, and turned to face me again. He then picked up the greasy napkin and wrapped it around my semi-flaccid cock, quickly bringing it back to life as he slathered it with natural lubricant. After my cock was covered with roast beef grease, he used the napkin to wipe behind his balls, lubricating his ass hole as best he could before he turned and bent over the bed.

I stepped behind him, grabbed his hips, and pressed the head of my grease-slickened cock against his tight little hole. As I pressed forward, Carnegie pressed backward, slowly opening to me. Soon I had the entire length of my cock buried in his ass. I drew back until only my cock head remained inside him before I pushed forward yet again.

Carnegie was soft but not doughy, his pale skin bruising easily as I gripped him and drilled into his ass. I drew back and slammed my hips forward again and again, fucking him hard and fast until I couldn't hold back any longer. Again, I came, rapturously filling his ass with a second load of come.

I stood holding him for the longest time, until my cock finally quit spasming and began to deflate. I then pulled out of him, sat on the side of the bed, and watched as he masturbated in front of me.

When he finished, I pulled him into my narrow bed and we fell asleep wrapped tightly around one another—servant and employer's guest—remaining entwined until the cook returned to the house shortly before sunrise, New Year's Day, and woke us with the clanking of pans.

She fed the musicians breakfast before the groundskeeper took them to the train station and, over the next several hours, prepared dozens of eggs, many rashers of bacon, and several loaves of toast, while I in turn offered aspirin, coffee, and hair of the dog to the hungover young men who requested it. Carnegie departed first, and the other guests vacated the house in twos and threes, just as they had come. By midday all horseless carriages but Fairchild's were gone from the property, much to relief of the groundskeeper. The housekeeper was far less relived at the disappearance of Fairchild's guests when she saw the condition of the furnishings, especially when she saw all the stains of unknown origin that would require days of effort to eliminate.

I took Fairchild's breakfast to his room after the last of his guests had driven away, and I settled a short-legged tray over his lap so that he could eat in bed.

"They'll not top last night any time soon," he proclaimed. Outlandish parties and over-the-top affairs were a form of competition among Fairchild's social set, and he seemed confident that he had bested the others with his turn-of-the-century orgy.

"I'm not certain many of them will even remember last night, Mr. Fairchild," I said. We both well knew that memories were mutable things. "Their drink set you back a good bit."

With a wave of his hand, my employer dismissed my concern about the evening's expense, much as I knew he would. What he did not know was that I had paid for alcohol I'd not received, and the money kicked back from the liquor wholesaler had found its way into one of my private accounts. I'd not done as well with the foodstuffs— limited as I was by the cook's detailed shopping list and the necessity of having to shop in Connecticut rather than in the city, where I had an extensive network of like-minded suppliers—but I still managed to pocket a few dollars thanks to a heavy-thumbed butcher.

I left Fairchild to finish his breakfast alone, wondering as I walked out of his bedroom if the copious amounts of alcohol and the celebratory sex heralding the arrival of the new century had pushed from his memory the one event that had made it all possible.

Though I remained in Fairchild's employ for two more decades and through several dozen more parties, I finally left him in the early 1920s after I had milked hundreds of thousands of dollars from the household accounts and saw that his remaining bank balance could not much longer sustain his lifestyle. Soon after leaving his employ, I headed west to Hollywoodland and the booming film industry, where I thought a man of my ambition, predilections, and skills could easily find opportunities.

As I'd imagined would happen, Fairchild burned through the remains of his inheritance long before Black Friday and the Great Depression erased the wealth of his former social circle. The last I heard anything about him, he was trying to explain away an anonymous letter to the police that implicated him in the untimely death of his grandfather a great many years earlier, an event easily misremembered by at least one of the two living witnesses.

I had been the invisible hired help in the bathhouse's steam room, silent witness to the accident that killed Fairchild's grandfather. The two men had been arguing yet again about Fairchild's demand for an increased allowance, and the young man had pushed his grandfather backward. The old man lost his footing on the slick floor and hit his head on the corner of the wooden bench as he fell. I thought Fairchild would call for help, but he hesitated and knelt beside the old man, seemingly checking for vital signs. Once certain that his grandfather was dead, Fairchild slipped out of the steam room only a few steps ahead of me and was found in the communal bath fifteen minutes later when one of the other members found his grandfather's lifeless body.

The police interviewed all the bathhouse's members but didn't get around to the employees until the following day, after I'd already had time to speak with Fairchild, mention my years of experience running the households of the well-to-do, and describe for him the mutability of my memory.

The police ruled his grandfather's death an accident, Fairchild inherited the old man's entire estate, and shortly thereafter he hired me at a salary well above the going rate for someone of my experience. As soon as I realized how little Fairchild understood about money and how much he had inherited, I began to supplement that income.

But what of the parties teeming with young men of a certain predilection?

I never could have predicted how much I would enjoy them, even after I moved to Hollywoodland and financed them myself.

THE GIMP, THE VIG,
AND THE RING

I lifted Jimmy the Gimp by the lapels of his shirt and pushed him back against the brick wall. "You don't have the money," I said, "you know what I got to do."

"Give me a break," the little guy squealed. "I never been late before."

"I need the vig." The vig. The vigorish. The weekly interest due on the money Jimmy had borrowed to bet on a horse that suffered a coronary three strides from the starting gate.

He kicked his good shoe and his corrective shoe with the built-up sole against the brick wall, scuffing the heels. "I ain't got the money, but I can get it."

"How?"

"My momma's engagement ring. I can hock my momma's engagement ring."

"She's not going to like that."

"She won't know nothin'. She's got the Alzheimer's. I'll tell her she lost it."

I liked Jimmy—everybody liked Jimmy—but I had a

job to do. I lowered him to the pavement and followed him to the third-floor walk-up he shared with his mother. The hallway outside smelled of curry, cat piss and vomit. I waited while he went inside. I killed time by thinking about Chuck and wondering what he had planned for our dinner. I was relieved when Jimmy slipped out of the apartment a few minutes later and opened his fist to reveal the diamond solitaire his father had given his mother many years earlier.

We walked down the block to Salvatore's and the old man behind the counter gave Jimmy a fair price for the ring. Jimmy shoved the pawnshop ticket in his wallet and the cash in my hands. It was more than enough to cover the week's vig.

"Give it all to Big Tony," he said. "I want to bet the trifecta."

"You sure you want to do that?"

After Jimmy nodded, I folded the stack of Hamiltons in half and slipped them into my inside jacket pocket next to my iPhone. Then we went our separate ways.

I made two more stops that afternoon—at a convent and at a bakery—before I returned to Big Tony's office at the used-bookstore. I gave my boss all the money I had collected and added a hundred of my own to cover Chuck's vig. I told him what to do with the extra Jimmy the Gimp had given me.

Big Tony separated Jimmy's betting money from the collected vig and pushed it to the side of his desk. "Gimp's already called. Thinks he has inside information on a trifecta."

"You take the bet?"

"Damn right I took the bet."

If my boss had ever had a heart, it had long ago turned to stone. Maybe the last decent thing he'd ever done was give me a job when no one else wanted anything to do with me. I'd been a big, dumb jock, just smart enough to play defensive tackle in high school and junior college but caught with steroids in my possession after a couple of Big Twelve coaches started eyeballing me. Even though I repeatedly tested negative, nobody believed I'd been set up, and I left college without finishing the season or my degree.

Soon after that Big Tony had me running errands. Before long I was collecting his debts. Less than a year later I was wearing custom-tailored suits and had moved from my parents' basement to my own two-bedroom apartment in a rent-controlled building. I went from juco dropout to somebody respected around the neighborhood, all because I became Big Tony's debt collector, and that respect allowed me to live a lifestyle not usually viewed favorably by my business associates.

When I asked if Big Tony had anything else for me, he dismissed me with a wave of his hand.

"I need a new racket," I said as I threw my custom-tailored jacket over the back of the black leather recliner.

Chuck stuck his head out of the kitchen. He'd gotten his hair styled earlier that day, and the stylist had touched up his blond highlights. He asked, "What happened?"

I unclipped my tie and threw it over the jacket. "I shook down a nun with a gambling habit."

Chuck snickered. "What's a nun's gambling habit look like? I'll bet it's black with a white wimple."

"Should you be betting?"

"I guess not." Chastised, my lover ducked back into the kitchen.

I had met Chuck on the job, collecting vig from him on a weekly basis until we each realized what the other kept in his closet, hidden from the rest of the world. We became closer than we should have considering my job and his debt-load, but he had a passion for muscle men—real muscle men, not oiled-up steroid junkies—and I liked a man that didn't mind a few bruises when my lovemaking got rough. Soon enough he moved into my apartment, and I paid Chuck's vig as long as he avoided the ponies and attended Gamblers Anonymous. I realized I'd been snippy with him, so I stepped into the kitchen, leaned down to kiss his cheek, and apologized.

I told him I'd had a rough day.

"Mine was no cakewalk," Chuck said as he continued tossing the salad. Chuck was no small man, but even brushing up against six feet he was still three inches shorter than me and several dozen pounds lighter. He waved one hand toward the kitchen door. "Go. Freshen up. Everything will be on the table in a few minutes."

I had just finished in the bathroom when Chuck called me to the dinner table. He'd made Caesar salad, linguini with clams and garlic butter sauce, and a loaf of garlic bread. He opened a bottle of white wine and poured us each a glass.

Then, over dinner, he told me about his day selling advertising space for a morning newspaper that was hemorrhaging money and threatening layoffs, and I told him about my day collecting Big Tony's debts. I told him about the mechanic who charged customers for work he didn't do just to cover the weekly vig on his off-the-books business loan, about the baker who complained every week about not having enough dough even though the joke hadn't been funny the first time I'd heard it, about the nun who paid the vig on her gambling debts by skimming from the donation plates, and about Jimmy the Gimp.

Everybody knew Jimmy the Gimp was harmless, and Chuck asked, "You didn't hurt him, did you?"

I shook my head. I'd never actually hurt any of the people whose money I collected, though my size and a persistent, though entirely fictitious, rumor that I'd once used a welsher's head for batting practice certainly put the fear of God into many of them.

"Stealing from his mother is pretty low," Chuck said. "Maybe you should get him into GA. I'll be his sponsor."

"I don't think he's ready," I replied. "He hasn't sunk low enough yet."

Chuck understood how low one had to sink before joining GA. The reason Chuck had moved in with me and had joined Gamblers Anonymous—beyond our mutual attraction—is that he had lost his car and had found all his things, what hadn't already been picked over by the Dumpster divers and street people, on the curb when he returned home from work one evening. In addition to Chuck, I'd convinced two of Big Tony's other clients to give up the lifestyle, one because he'd fathered a son and the other because his wife needed chemotherapy. Big Tony wasn't pleased with my charity work, but the impact on his bottom line was negligible.

After dinner, Chuck cleared the table and filled the dishwasher while I changed into cross-training shoes, gray sweats, a wife-beater, and black weightlifting gloves. Then he changed into running shoes, shorts, and a pink T-shirt he'd received for participating in a Susan G. Komen Race for the Cure. I grabbed some bottled water, and we took the elevator to the basement.

The dank space had been divided into six storage areas that were little more than waist-high walls built of one-by-twos, with chicken wire the rest of the way to the ceiling. The storage spaces weren't secure by any means but half the building's residents each paid an extra two hundred a month just to have use of one of them.

Chuck had helped me convert mine to a workout room, complete with a weight bench, free weights, exercise mat, treadmill, heavy bag and a speed bag. He usually accompanied me when I worked out, not because he would be of any help if I dropped the weights, but because seeing me pump iron turned him on and he was always primed to finish the workout in the privacy of our bedroom.

A single bare bulb dangling from the ceiling illuminated our storage area and a small fan in the corner helped circulate the smell of damp basement and sweaty men. We turned both on.

Chuck joined me for stretching exercises. After we limbered up, he jogged on the treadmill while I worked with the free weights. I'm not a bodybuilder. I have no interest in building show muscle, oiling up, and posing near naked before a theater full of Charles Atlas wannabes, horny groupies of all genders and steroid pushers. I maintain my size and strength for my job, relying on my imposing physique more than anything else to intimidate.

My workouts consisted of heavy days and light days, and that night was a heavy day. I put three hundred pounds on the barbell and bench-pressed three sets of five reps; squatted three sets of five reps with four hundred pounds on the barbell; power cleaned five sets of two hundred fifty pounds; and finished with ten hundred-pound curls for each arm. My wife-beater was soaked with sweat but I was barely breathing heavy when I finished with the weights.

After draining one of the bottled waters without a pause, I pulled on twelve-ounce boxing gloves and worked the speed bag with a steady *rat-a-tat-tat*. When Chuck finished his jog, I switched to the heavy bag, and he leaned into it while I pummeled it from the opposite side.

I should have been concentrating on my fists and how they landed against the bag because someday I was actually going to get into a fight, but I kept sneaking peeks at my lover. His blue eyes were half closed, and his partially erect cock tented the front of his shorts. Because I was paying too much attention to Chuck's package, a roundhouse punch missed the bag and caught him in the upper arm.

Chuck's eyes snapped open, and he stumbled

backward, releasing his hold on the heavy bag as he went. The bag swung forward and smacked into me with no noticeable effect. I asked, "You okay?"

"Sure," he said as he rubbed his arm.

I peeled off my gloves, hooked one hand behind his head, and pulled him close. I covered his mouth with mine and gave him a deep, tongue-tangling kiss. When it ended, I said, "Let's go upstairs."

One of the first things I'd done after moving into the apartment was remodel the bathroom, tearing out the claw-foot bathtub and replacing it with a custom-built shower appropriate for a man my size—a man my size who liked company. Chuck and I stripped off our sweaty workout clothes, shoved them into the wicker hamper, and slipped into the shower.

He grabbed the bath mitt first, lathered it up with lavender-scented antibacterial body wash and began scrubbing my back and my chest. He worked his way down my body until he was kneeling on the tile floor in front of me, the warm water cascading over us from two separate showerheads and my erect cock bobbing in front of his face.

He used the bath mitt to scrub my heavy ball sac as he leaned forward and took the head of my cock into his mouth. He hooked his teeth behind the spongy soft glans and then bathed my cock head with his tongue.

I reached down and took his head in my hands, holding it as I pushed my cock deep into his oral cavity.

He accepted every inch—something no other man I'd been with had been able to do—before I pulled back and pressed forward again. I moved my hips slowly at first, and then with increasing speed. Soon my ball sac was slapping against Chuck's chin, and it slowly tightened up the closer I was to orgasm.

When I finally came, I came hard, firing a thick wad of hot spunk against the back of Chuck's throat. He swallowed every drop and then licked my cock clean before I pulled him to his feet. The workout had turned me on, too, and even though I'd just come my cock only softened for a moment.

I spun Chuck around so that he was facing the tiled wall. We don't keep any lube in the shower, so I grabbed antibacterial soap and dribbled it down his ass crack. He bent forward, shoving his ass back toward me and I pressed my cock head against his soapy sphincter. Then I grabbed his hips and pressed forward, driving my cock into him.

Chuck braced himself against the tile wall with one hand and wrapped the fingers of his free hand around his erect cock, matching his fist pumps to my rhythm. I came first, slamming into him and holding his hips so tight I bruised them for the second time that month. Then he came, spewing spunk on the tile wall that was quickly washed away by the cascading water.

We finished our shower a bit more sedately than we began it, wrapping matching terry-cloth bathrobes around ourselves and then sitting in the living room and finishing the bottle of wine Chuck had opened at dinner.

When we finally went to bed, I fell asleep with my arms wrapped around Chuck, holding him tight as if I was afraid he would escape during the night, knowing that everything was right with the world when I had him in my arms.

I woke up alone: Chuck had already gone for the day when I finally pushed myself out of bed and into the shower. He'd left half a pot of coffee made from freshly ground beans and I downed it before I dressed in a crisply pressed white shirt, clip-on tie and a suit that Chuck had picked up at the dry cleaner's on his way home the previous day. Then I checked my iPhone, saw that I had no messages and made my way to the first pickup of the day.

Time disappeared quickly. I was thinking of lunch at the Pasta Barn, having already collected the weekly vig from four of Big Tony's regulars, when my iPhone rang. I dug in my jacket pocket for it.

As soon as I answered, Big Tony shouted in my ear, "The son-of-a-bitch hit the trifecta and just walked out of here with ten Gs."

"Who?"

"Jimmy the Gimp, that's who."

"You let him leave with all that money?"

"What was I supposed to do?" Big Tony yelled. "I got a reputation. I pay my debts just like I expect people to pay theirs. That's what Jimmy did. I got my cut and then he gimped out of here with ten Gs of my money."

"What do you want me to do about it?"

"Find the son-of-a-bitch and convince him to lay off some of that money."

After Big Tony disconnected the call, I slid the iPhone back into my jacket pocket alongside two thousand dollars I'd already collected. Instead of visiting the bartender with a hard-on for sports betting, I changed direction and headed back toward Jimmy the Gimp's neighborhood.

I found him by accident when I heard someone shouting as I walked past the mouth of an alley two blocks from Salvatore's. When I turned and entered the alley, I found three guys putting the squeeze on Jimmy behind a foul-smelling Dumpster. The little guy tried to give as good as he got—his heavy corrective shoe connected with one guy's nut sac and drove him to his knees—but he was outnumbered and one of the guys held a length of pipe that he was using to play stickball with Jimmy's noggin.

Before I could reach them, Jimmy was on the ground, curled in a ball, and he'd stopped resisting. One of the three punks tore Jimmy's jacket off of him.

I grabbed the nearest guy and slammed his head against the recently emptied Dumpster. The Dumpster clanged like a church bell and the punk dropped to his knees. I swung at the next guy, missing with a roundhouse left when he stepped inside of it. He grabbed my tie and brought his knee up toward my groin, but my clip-on tie came off in his hand and he lost his balance. A right uppercut to his chin sent him to the ground with his pal, leaving only the guy with the pipe to deal with.

He took one look up at me, dropped the pipe and ran

with Jimmy's jacket still gripped tightly in one hand. His two buddies scrambled to their feet and followed. I thought about giving chase but figured they could outrun me. I spent too much time in weight training and, despite Chuck's encouragement, not enough time doing cardio.

I knew Big Tony would put word out on the street and that by the end of the week we'd know the names of three punks flashing wads of cash they had no logical right to, so I turned my attention to Jimmy the Gimp.

He hadn't moved.

I sat beside him, not concerned about the filth staining the seat of my suit pants, and cradled the Gimp's head in my lap.

"The ring," he said, slurring his words. Blood trickled from his ear. "I was going to get my momma's ring."

That was the last thing Jimmy the Gimp said before he closed his eyes forever. I took the pawnshop ticket from his wallet and retrieved his mother's engagement ring from Salvatore's, using my own money because the three punks had gotten away with Jimmy's winnings.

Then I walked down the block and up two flights of stairs. The hallway outside the Gimp's apartment still smelled of curry, cat piss and vomit, and I tapped lightly on the apartment door.

A moment later a weathered old woman wearing mismatched shoes and a faded blue housedress that hadn't been properly fastened jerked the door open and stared up at me. "Do I know you?"

"No, ma'am," I said, "but I knew Jimmy." I handed her the engagement ring. "He said you lost this."

After she took the ring from my hand and put it on her finger, I turned and walked away. The police would come soon enough to tell her what had happened to her son.

I needed Chuck. I needed him to hold me and tell me everything was going to be okay. I pulled out my iPhone and dialed his number.

THE GUNSEL, THE NANCE, AND THE REDHEADED ROOSTER

The gunsel's Tommy gun burped, and two of Risotto's boys collapsed in a heap of human marinara sauce. Neither of their Roscoes had cleared leather.

The baby-faced blond smiled and rubbed the front of his gray wool trousers with his left hand, leaving his right index finger on the chopper's trigger in case the wooden door behind the dead men opened unexpectedly. The gunsel's cock was rigid as a railroad spike and just as long when fully erect. If he didn't do something to relieve the pressure soon, he would come all over the inside of his silk boxers.

The door had developed lead measles and was wet with blood. The gunsel stepped around the stiffs and tapped the chopper's muzzle against it. "Open the door, Billy."

He waited until he heard the latch being lifted. Then he threw his shoulder against the door, surprising the dark-haired nance on the other side and knocking him backward against the desk. One of two matching accounting ledgers that had been open on the desk fell to the floor.

"Where's Risotto?"

"He ain't here, Kid," the nance insisted. He was pale and sweating, and his brown eyes darted back and forth as if he couldn't focus. He wore a white shirt buttoned at the cuffs and the fingers of one hand were stained with ink. "He ain't been here all week."

"Why'd you take a powder, Billy? What'd Risotto promise you?"

"I see you got a redheaded rooster wants to crow," Billy said nervously, changing the subject before the gunsel went too far off the track. "Let me take care of that for you, Kid. You know you like it when I do."

The room had no windows, no way in or out save for the door. The gunsel crossed the room and leaned against the desk, his ass atop the remaining ledger, facing the open doorway. The nance dropped to his knees and unbuttoned the gunsel's baggy trousers. He reached through the open fly, through the opening of the gunsel's blue silk boxers, and released the gunsel's erect cock.

"It's so hard, Kid," the nance said before he took the head of the gunsel's cock in his mouth. His tongue painted the swollen cock head and he licked away the first few drops of pre-come.

The nance bobbed his head forward, taking half the length into his mouth before pulling back. He teeth caught on the mushroom cap, and then he bobbed his head forward again.

The gunsel was impatient. He grabbed the back of

Billy's head with his left hand and shoved the full length of his redheaded rooster into the smaller man's mouth. He still held the Tommy gun in his right hand, and he watched the door as he drew back and thrust forward again and again, face fucking the smaller man.

The nance accepted every one of the Kid's powerful thrusts, just as he'd done many times before at the rooming house where they had lived across the hall from one another until the nance lammed off, stiffing the old broad who ran the joint a week's rent.

The gunsel pounded into the nance's face harder and faster and when his redheaded rooster crowed his trigger finger twitched. Lead peppered the wall next to the open doorway at the same time he fired a thick wad of hot spunk against the back of the nance's throat.

Billy swallowed every drop of the Kid's come and licked his slowly softening cock clean. When the gunsel's redheaded rooster finally stopped spasming in his mouth, Billy released his oral grip on it and shoved the gunsel's limp cock back into his trousers.

The Kid grabbed Billy's arm and pulled him to his feet. Then he pulled back one of the nance's shirtsleeves to reveal the needle tracks on the smaller man's arm.

"Risotto do this to you?"

"It's nothing, Kid," Billy insisted. "I can quit any time."

"Don't lie to me." The gunsel backhanded Billy, knocking his former lover to the floor. "It cost me a double sawbuck to find out where you'd got to and now I wished I ain't laid out the dough. I been played for a sap."

He pointed the business end of the Thompson submachine gun at the nance and but didn't squeeze the trigger. Instead, he awkwardly buttoned his trousers with his left hand and then tore apart the desk until he found Billy's sewing kit. He laid the fixings on the desktop and smashed them with the butt of his Tommy gun.

"You ain't the man you was," the Kid said. "You ain't nothing now."

After he finished, the Kid made his way out of the warehouse. When he reached the street, he jumped in his flivver and faded.

The Kid stopped at a hash house for Adam and Eve on a raft, a cuppa Joe, and a long think. He'd been able to get the drop on the two mugs at the warehouse because they hadn't been there to keep people out but to keep Billy in. What had the nance been doing for Risotto that he would require babysitters?

He ankled his way to the Ameche and dropped a dime. When Bertha, the old broad who ran the rooming house, picked up the other end of the line, the gunsel asked two questions. After he heard the answers, he left a half on the counter for the waitress and returned to his flivver. He reloaded his Tommy gun and then drove downtown.

Speakeasies littered the city, offering everything from bathtub gin to untaxed Canadian imports, but only one served men who liked men. The men inside this speakeasy weren't Capones or North Side Gang, Risotto's boys or O'Malley's boyos. They shared a secret that usually transcended their particular employment affiliations.

The baby-faced blond gunsel rapped on the steel door until a dark eye filled the peephole. After he gave the password, the door opened.

He stepped inside, and the gorilla who worked the door frisked him, spending a little too much time scrambling his eggs. The gunsel slapped the gorilla's paw aside and stared him down.

Then he made his way to the bar and ordered a straight shot of Canadian whiskey. While he waited for his drink, the gunsel lit a gasper and drew the harsh, unfiltered smoke deep into his lungs. He exhaled it through his nostrils. Then he threw back the first shot and ordered a second.

He looked around. The place was filled with a bunch of daisies, and he saw the man he wanted standing at the far end of the bar, a man with a cauliflower ear. He walked up behind Eddie the Ear and dropped a hand on his shoulder. "Buy you a drink?"

The other man turned, gave the Kid a look over and said, "Sure."

The gunsel held up two fingers and the bartender brought two shots.

"Do you know who I am?" the Kid asked.

"I seen you around," Eddie the Ear said. He picked up his shot glass and downed his drink. "You're one of O'Malley's boyos, ain't you?"

"Yeah." The Kid downed his own drink, his third since arriving at the speakeasy. "They got rooms in the back where we can talk private. You interested?"

Eddie held up his shot glass. "Buy me another?"

The Kid bought a bottle and carried it and two clean glasses to the back.

Half a dozen private rooms lined the rear wall of the speakeasy and were accessible through a narrow hallway with a skinny shine sitting on a high stool at one end and a door leading to the alley at the other. He handed the darkie a half and received the key to room three. The room, like all the others, was sparsely furnished—a single bed covered in a thin cotton sheet, a waist-high stool, a nightstand with a lamp, hooks on the wall to hang clothing, and a partially used jar of petroleum jelly.

The gunsel had brought Eddie the Ear into the room so they could talk privately, but Eddie had other expectations. While the gunsel poured two shots, Eddie undressed.

The Kid was still hyped up from giving two men a dirt nap earlier that evening and his drug-addled former lover had only temporarily satisfied him. When he saw Eddie's naked body, his redheaded rooster stretched its neck, preparing to crow again.

The Kid peeled off his jacket and hung it on one of the hooks. He sat on the side of the bed to remove his shoes and socks, then stood again and pushed his braces from his shoulders so that he could remove his shirt and undershirt. He hung his baggy trousers on the hook next to his jacket and finally peeled off his boxers.

When the gunsel's redheaded rooster finally sprang free, Eddie's eyes widened in appreciation and he said, "Well, cock-a-doodle-doo!"

Eddie reached for the Kid's cock, but the Kid wasn't

interested in foreplay. He spun Eddie around and bent him over the waist-high stool. He grabbed the jar of petroleum jelly, pried it open, and two-fingered out a glob of the lubricant.

He slathered some of it on his cock and worked the rest into Eddie's bum hole. He massaged his companion's tight sphincter until he could slip in one slick finger. A moment later he slipped in a second finger.

After he pulled his fingers away, he pressed his redheaded rooster between the other man's cheeks. Then he thrust his hips forward and drove his cock deep into Eddie's keister.

He grabbed Eddie's hips as he drew back and drove forward again and again. By then Eddie the Ear's cock had grown just as hard as the Kid's. The gunsel reached around and grabbed Eddie's nail-pounder with his petroleum jelly-slicked hand and jerked off his partner while he pounded into him from behind.

Eddie came first, spitting spunk all over the stool.

Then the Kid's redheaded rooster crowed for the second time that night as the gunsel slammed into Eddie one last time and fired hot spunk into the other man's keister.

They remained connected for more than a minute as they waited for the gunsel's rooster to stop crowing and withdraw.

After they finished, the gunsel dressed and lit another gasper. He drew in a deep breath of unfiltered cigarette smoke and asked, "You know Billy Hansen?"

Eddie shook his head. He sat on the edge of the bed,

his nail-pounder having deflated into a limp noodle that hung between his thighs. He seemed in no hurry to dress.

"You convinced Billy to vacate his room at Bertha's, take up residence in one of Risotto's back rooms."

Eddie the Ear shook his head. "You're tooting the wrong ringer."

"I don't think so," the gunsel told him. "Bertha saw you visit Billy one afternoon. That night he made like a ghost and faded."

"Wasn't me."

The gunsel's hand snapped out and clapped Eddie's cauliflower ear. Once. Twice. Three times before Eddie winced. "Don't lie to me. That ear's a giveaway, Eddie."

Eddie cupped one hand over his deformed ear and turned his good ear toward the gunsel.

"How'd you convince him to go to Risotto?"

"I told him the coppers were planning to raid the rooming house. I said a pretty boy like him wouldn't stand a chance in the big house and that you wouldn't stand up for him. I convinced him that Risotto would."

The Kid crushed the butt of the gasper under the toe of his shoe. "Why would Billy think Risotto would protect him from the coppers?"

"Because Risotto knew his daddy, Big Jim Hansen."

Big Jim Hansen had run Central Illinois with an iron fist until Johnny Torrio, two years before he turned the Chicago Outfit over to Al Capone, had a pair of torpedoes give Hansen a fatal case of lead poisoning.

"Big Jim Hansen was his daddy?" The Kid hesitated. "He never said."

"I don't think he wanted anybody to know."

"Why did Risotto send you?"

"Because I knew Billy from when he was in diapers." Eddie turned his deformed ear toward the gunsel and pointed at it. "His daddy done this to me."

"So, why'd Risotto want him?"

"Billy does the books at The Diamond Exchange and Risotto has a truckload of liquor money he needs to launder."

The Kid remembered the matching accounting ledgers that had been on the desk when he'd burst into the office where he found Billy. "I saw Billy's arm. He's stitched up. Risotto put him on the needle?"

"He did that to himself. Risotto just keeps him threaded."

The chatter of a pair of Thompson submachine guns interrupted their conversation, startling both men. The background noise of a busy speakeasy—idle conversation, bottles clinking against glasses, chairs scraping across the floor—turned to dead silence when the choppers quit spewing lead.

Through the door they heard someone shout, "Where's the Kid?"

The gunsel recognized Risotto's voice. When no one responded to the question, he opened the door a crack and looked up and down the hallway. The shine at the far end saw him but didn't react.

The Kid slipped out of the room and had just made it to the exit when he heard someone say, "The Kid's in back."

He pushed through the door and headed down the alley. Another one of Risotto's torpedoes was standing guard in front of his flivver, but facing the entrance to the speakeasy, not the alley. The Kid was on him in a flash. He snapped the mug's neck and tore the chopper from the dead man's hand. Then he reached under the front seat of his flivver for his Tommy gun and turned to face the alley with the butt of a chopper resting on each hip.

The first of the three torpedoes with Risotto rounded the corner and the gunsel cut him in half with bursts from both guns. As if he had a death wish, the gunsel ankled his way toward the alley entrance.

The muzzle of a Tommy gun rounded the corner. The gunsel sent a burst from one of his, shattering brick all around the muzzle, and the other gun drew back.

The gunsel stepped into the mouth of the alley. He filled it with lead mosquitoes that ricocheted from one wall to the other. Another of Risotto's torpedoes dropped dead.

"You want me, Risotto?" the Kid shouted. "Here I am!"

From behind a garbage bin Risotto shouted back. "Does O'Malley know you've gone off the rails, Kid?"

"This is between you and me, Risotto."

"We didn't find Billy until it was too late," Risotto shouted. "He killed himself. He left a note, said it was your fault."

"I didn't stitch him up," the gunsel shouted. "That was your doing."

Risotto's remaining torpedo stepped out from a doorway and unloaded his chopper in the Kid's direction.

Brick chips peppered the gunsel's face and ricocheting lead imbedded in his left bicep. He winced.

The Kid's Tommy guns burped in return, halving the torpedo.

"You stitched him up, Kid," Risotto continued. "I just gave him the sewing kit. He loved you, but you just used him and he knew it. You don't love anybody but yourself and he needed a way to escape from the pain."

"Why dope?"

"It's the future, Kid, and you're the past."

The gunsel felt the cold circle of a revolver barrel against the base of his skull and heard a hammer being cocked into place. Risotto'd had another torpedo the gunsel hadn't accounted for. The Kid was about to die, and all because of some nance he'd been banging.

He squeezed the triggers of both Tommy guns, filling the alley with ricocheting lead, and never heard the bullet that bought him a wooden kimono.

WHAT A RUSH

Rush Week, which began the Monday before the new semester started, was crazy, with every fraternity and sorority sponsoring tables in the student union building and hundreds of would-be pledges trooping like lemmings from one table to the next. I was one of the lemmings, doing my best to learn everything I could—which wasn't much—about each fraternity and to learn when each house would be hosting smokers that week.

I desired the Greek life, seeing it as a stepping-stone to the life I wanted for myself rather than the life I might face if I were forced to return home following college graduation. My family lived in the wrong small town, the poorest of a cluster of three that sent their children to a centrally located high school, and no amount of education, effort, or desire would change that if I returned. Only by whitewashing my upbringing and by making connections with the sons and daughters of the moneyed elite would I have any chance of breaking away from a past predetermined by the socio-economic status consigned upon me at birth. That's why I had studied hard and worked harder throughout high school, graduating with a GPA just shy of 4.0, and that only because the PE teacher hadn't thought highly of those students usually picked last for team sports. I'd been able to choose between several universities, weighing financial aid packages designed to attract academic high achievers against the cachet of having a particular school's name on my diploma, the probability of making life-long connections with the right people while attending the school, and the matriculation rates of my high school's previous graduates at each university.

Tuesday afternoon, we lemmings trooped from house to house along fraternity row—a several-block-long stretch of mansions converted to fraternity houses, sorority houses, and other university-centric establishments— working our way from the largest, most ornate houses closest to campus to the smaller, less appealing houses farther away. Though there were many other considerations for desiring membership in a particular fraternity, proximity to campus was one of the most obvious status symbols, and membership in one of the four fraternities and two sororities housed within the first block of fraternity row was highly desired by those who placed status at the top of their list. Most of the members of the close-by fraternities were handsome, moneyed, overachievers whose successes post-graduation more often came from family connections than their own hard work.

I had the look and the grades, but I didn't have the money. What I did have was a bit of inside knowledge about the president of one of the top four fraternities, a guy who graduated from my high school three years before me and was beginning his senior year at the university as I was beginning my freshman year. Kyle Dennison didn't remember me, but I had no reason to think he would. I'd grown several inches, my acne had cleared up, and I'd learned to dress appropriately by studying men's fashion magazines and trolling resale shops. I found myself face-to-face with him at the third smoker of the afternoon, having already visited two other fraternities where I had taken house tours, shot pool, played foosball, eaten snacks, and practiced my pitch. I wanted fraternity members to remember me as interested but not desperate, and by the time I was face-to-face with Kyle, I felt confident that I had my pitch perfected.

I introduced myself with my middle name—Marshall—rather than my first name, a name not often given to boys and all the more memorable because my parents had saddled me with it to please a long-dead great-grandfather. My last name—Smith—was so generic I needn't ever bother hiding it.

Kyle shook my outstretched hand, welcomed me to the frat house, and told me about some of the charity work and community service projects they were planning for the year, making the fraternity sound as if it were populated by angelic cherubs rather than the spoiled rich kids I knew them to be. As I shook his hand, I told Kyle how delighted I was to meet him, how much I had enjoyed meeting the other members, and how pleased I was to learn of their community involvement. I didn't tell him that his touch was sending blood rushing to my crotch and that it took mental images of slaughtered livestock to prevent myself from having an erection.

"Get yourself something to eat," he said, before moving on to glad-hand another potential pledge.

Unlike some of the lesser fraternities that served little more than chips and dip, Kyle's fraternity, and the others nearest the university, put on a big spread. The highlights at Kyle's house included shrimp cocktail and a chef carving thin slices of roast beef. I snacked, exchanged polite conversation with a variety of active members, and then moved on to the next house, remaining just long enough at each to make an impression but not so long that I might wear out my welcome the way some of the less sophisticated freshmen did.

That night I returned to fraternity row for the parties, once again making certain I was seen by the decision makers at several fraternities, but not embarrassing myself by drinking excessively or participating in juvenile antics. During a brief conversation with Kyle, I mentioned my plan to major in business just as he was majoring in business, laughed at his joke about English majors, and lightly rested my fingers on his forearm just long enough for him to react, pulling away before anyone else noticed. I knew his gaze followed me when I walked away, and I wondered if I might have been too subtle.

There were more smokers Wednesday afternoon, so I finished visiting the fraternities, ensuring that I left a good impression at a few of the lesser houses in case my plan to pledge Kyle's fraternity somehow failed. That night I remained in my dorm room between eight and ten p.m., when lemming-like rushees like myself were expected to welcome active members of various fraternities into their rooms for a little Q&A. Active members from five fraternities visited me and asked about my background, my interests, and my goals for college and beyond. I aced their questions and responded with a few of my own, sending each group of actives on their way satisfied with their visit, but I paced nervously as ten p.m. approached and actives from Kyle's fraternity had yet to knock on my door.

I was about to give up hope when they finally arrived at two minutes past.

"Sorry we're late," Kyle apologized as I ushered the three of them into my dorm room. "It's been a long night."

My room wasn't designed to accommodate large groups, so Denny and Chad sat in the only two chairs while Kyle and I sat on my bed, an arrangement I orchestrated in order to put certain thoughts in Kyle's mind.

They asked many of the same questions as the other fraternities, and my answers were nearly identical. The only variation was Kyle's reaction when I named my hometown, a place so insignificant that no one but residents of the tri-town area knew of it, and I saw the recognition in Kyle's eyes. For the next several minutes, as Denny and Chad continued their questioning, Kyle studied me closely, perhaps trying to determine if he should know me or know of me.

They seemed satisfied with my answers when they finally stood to leave at twenty past ten, and I stepped with them to the door. Denny and Chad exited first, and I put my hand on the small of Kyle's back, out of sight of the other two members of his fraternity, my fingers grazing the upper swell of his tight buttocks. He stiffened at the touch but did not otherwise react as my hand slid lower before I pulled it away.

"We're having an invitational tomorrow night," Chad said. "You should come."

As Kyle turned to face me, I stared into his pale blue eyes. "Should I?" I asked. "Should I come?"

After he nodded, I promised I would.

I didn't attend any of the Thursday smokers and arrived fashionably late to the party at Kyle's fraternity house. A dozen or so other rushees had arrived before me and a few more arrived after, so I knew the process of winnowing candidates was in full swing. I mingled, moving from group to group, discussing the things young men discuss when they gather together. I soon learned which professors to avoid, which bars were lax about checking IDs, and which Tri-Delt never seemed to draw her curtains before changing clothes. I couldn't care less about naked Tri-Delts, but I feigned interest when Chad described the size of her breasts.

Kyle caught me alone in the dining room as I was refilling my glass from the crystal punch bowl. "I should know your people."

"You do," I admitted.

"We should have been in school together."

"We were."

"Why don't I know you?"

"You never looked at me twice," I said, "but I know

about you. I saw you and Steven Harper in the Harper's stock pond the summer before you came here."

Kyle's eyes widened, but before he could respond, Denny stumbled into the dining room. He'd been drinking, spiking his punch with Jack Daniel's, and apparently couldn't hold his liquor. Kyle grabbed Denny's arm and guided him into the bathroom. While they were busy, I made appropriate farewells and slipped out of the party. Then I walked down fraternity row to one of the two other invitationals at which I was expected. After staying only long enough to ensure that I left a positive impression at each of the two invitationals I visited after leaving Kyle's fraternity house, I managed to turn in for the night at a reasonable hour.

The next morning Kyle caught me outside my room returning from the dormitory's communal shower with just a towel around my waist. He invited himself in and sat on the bed next to me.

"It's not looking good," Kyle said. He rested one hand on my knee. "There are some other guys we're looking at real *hard*."

"I'm certain you are," I responded, realizing that the inside information he was giving me—whether true or not—was a bit of dirty rushing. Fortunately, I could play dirty, too. "As hard as you looked at Steven Harper when you two went skinny dipping."

"So, you know what I want, Beverly," Kyle said as he slipped his hand under the towel. He had done his homework overnight, learning the name my family had bestowed on me and which had caused me to defend myself against all manner of taunting and misunderstandings during my formative years.

I said, "I'm surprised no one else does."

He shrugged. "I'll marry a Tri-Delt, have two kids, and keep a friend or two on the side."

"Like Harper?"

"He's history," Kyle explained. His fingers found my freshly washed scrotum and he cupped my balls in his hand. "He was a fling, nothing more."

My cock stiffened as he massaged my balls, and the towel tented in my lap. Kyle wrapped his fist around my cock and jerked me off, his strokes hard and fast, and before I could stop myself, I came. As my sexual effluent soaked the towel, Kyle drew his hand away. I stood and peeled off the towel, used it to wipe away the last few drops of come, and tossed it on the floor.

Kyle leaned back on the bed, rested on his elbows, and watched me clean myself. I could see the bulge in his chinos, his cock straining for release, and I accommodated his needs by unzipping his fly. I knew what I would see when I helped him remove his pants and toss them aside, but I had never seen his long, thick erection so close. When I'd first noticed Kyle fucking Steven Harper at the Harper Pond, I'd watched them through the scope of my hunting rifle, and each subsequent time, once I'd determined their twice-weekly assignations, I'd watched them through my father's binoculars. By then I knew, but had not acted upon, my own sexual desires, and that summer was the first time I realized exactly what it was that aroused me.

Kyle's cock rose from a closely trimmed triangle of blond pubic hair, the purplish head crowned with a glistening bead of pre-come. I knelt beside the bed, positioned myself between Kyle's widespread thighs, and took the head of his cock in my mouth. I sucked away the drop of pre-come and then slowly drew the length of his stiff shaft into my oral cavity.

I couldn't quite take it all in before I drew back and caught my teeth on his spongy glans. As I took his cock into my mouth a second time and then a third, Kyle sat up. He put his hands on either side of my head and held it as he moved his hips forward and back, fucking my face. The faster and harder he thrust his cock into my oral cavity, the farther he rose from the bed, until he was on his feet in an awkward crouch, his ball sac slapping my chin, his short pubic hair scratching my lips, his breath coming in ragged gasps. I felt Kyle tense as he thrust forward one last time, and then his cock erupted within my mouth, sending wad after thick wad of hot come against the back of my throat. I couldn't swallow fast enough and some of it dribbled from the corners of my mouth, dripping onto the wadded-up towel at my knees.

When Kyle finished coming in my mouth, he pulled away and sat back on the bed, his wet cock a slowly shrinking reminder of what we'd just done. I wiped my mouth and chin with the towel and neither of us spoke until Kyle reached for his chinos. "I'll talk to the other actives tonight," he said. "I'll put in a good word. That's all I can promise."

After he dressed, Kyle invited me to that night's

closed party at the frat house, my last opportunity to impress the actives and secure a bid. I knew I already had Kyle's vote, and I knew as president of the chapter he would have plenty of influence on the other members, but I still had to play the game as if I didn't share Kyle's secret.

That night I arrived at the frat house a few minutes after the closed party began, neither the first nor the last rushee to arrive, and I soon learned that the field of rushees had been narrowed to nine. Once again, I handled myself well, offended no one, and left at the end of the evening with hearty handshakes from Denny, Chad, and several of the other actives.

All the campus fraternities and sororities spent Saturday selecting which rushees to bid the following day. For some Greek organizations, the choices were simple, for others the decisions were difficult and took hours of deliberation. I had no idea what kind of deliberations went on at Kyle's house, but when I returned to my room Sunday afternoon after chapel, I found two bids awaiting me. The first came from one of the lesser fraternities located near the far end of fraternity row, an organization that would be quite pleased to have me join because the average I.Q. of the house would raise seven points just by my presence. The second, from Kyle's fraternity, was accompanied by a private dinner invitation for later that evening.

I smiled. I had exactly what I wanted.

But I wondered if I could get more, and I was still wondering when I met Kyle at a dimly lit hotel restaurant downtown. Over lobster tails, he congratulated me on my bid and suggested we further celebrate after dinner. I let him know I shared the same thought, and I was not surprised when I learned he had already rented a room.

Once we had the door locked behind us, Kyle wasn't shy. He backed me against a wall and kissed me. Our tongues met and his tasted of lobster and baked Alaska and coffee. As our kiss lengthened and deepened, his fingers fumbled open the buttons, buckle, and zipper that kept my clothes on, and he soon had me naked and sprawled face-down on the king-size bed. After he peeled off his own clothes, Kyle grabbed a brand-new tube of lube from the nightstand, squeezed lube into his hand, and massaged it into my ass crack. I rose up on all fours, positioning my knees near the edge of the bed. After a moment, he pressed the tip of one lube-slickened finger against my sphincter and I slowly opened to the pressure. He slathered more lube into my ass crack as he slid his finger into and out, and soon he was able to slide a second finger into me.

"Quit teasing me," I whispered hoarsely, and he replaced his fingers with the head of his cock.

I pushed back as he grabbed my hips and pushed forward, and soon the entire length of Kyle's cock was buried in my ass. I didn't tell him, because the less information he had about me the better, but he was my first, and I reveled in every stroke as he drew back and pushed forward. He fucked me hard, and he fucked me fast and he came with a roar as he fired hot sum up my ass, collapsed on top of me, and flattened me against the bed. I had to pleasure myself when he caught his breath and rolled off me, but I didn't care.

He watched me jerk off and waited until I finished before he said anything. "I expect you to keep our arrangement quiet. Can you do that?"

I thought for a moment, even though I already knew what I planned to say. "I might need a little help keeping up appearances," I said. "I wouldn't want to diminish the fraternity's image by ever appearing less than my best."

"I think that can be arranged," Kyle said. "I've already talked to my father about our situation. You should expect to receive a very healthy scholarship from the bank back home. It'll get you through the year. Spend it wisely because after that, you're on your own."

We fucked twice more that evening, once in bed and again in the shower when we were supposed to be cleaning up. Then, because we had driven separate cars, I left him at the hotel and returned to my dorm room, where I slept soundly for the first time since Rush Week began.

Monday was the semester's first day of class, which kept me busy either in class or in the bookstore buying the outrageously expensive pile of books I needed that semester, and Tuesday, the first day rushees were allowed to pledge, I officially pledged Kyle's fraternity, one of only five to received bids.

By then I had already started listening closely to my fraternity brothers, hoping to find someone to replace Kyle's friendship and generosity after he graduated at the end of the year. After all, it isn't just who you know, sometimes it's *what* you know about who you know that allows you to get ahead.

THE HITTER AND THE STALL

I clamped my hand around the man's wrist and squeezed until he whimpered and released my wallet, letting it drop back into my hip pocket. Without loosening my grip, I turned to face him. The subway riders crowded around us were oblivious to what was happening mere inches from them, and I spoke softly to keep it that way. "That's a terrible dip."

The slender young blond grimaced but also kept his voice low. "You're hurting me."

"You're lucky I don't break your wrist." I showed him his wallet. "Or keep this."

Astonishment overcame the blond's pain. "How did you do that?"

I flipped his wallet open and thumbed his driver's license out far enough that I could read his name and address. Then I thumbed it back into place, tucked his wallet into his shirt pocket and patted it lightly. "I have the gift, Sean."

The subway slid to a halt and the doors opened. I slipped out with the other exiting passengers before the amateur pickpocket realized I'd released my grip on his wrist. I tried to fade into the crowd, but he followed me anyhow and caught me at the top of the stairs. He grabbed my jacket sleeve. "Teach me."

I examined Sean more carefully this time. At least twenty years my junior, he wasn't big enough for strong-arm work. Even so, there was a certain spark of intelligence in his pale blue eyes, something I'd not often seen in the young punks more interested in snatch-and-grab opportunities than in the subtle art of dipping. Sean wasn't bad on the eyes, either, and I suspected I could first teach him to be a stall, the same way an older hitter named Joey "Fingers" Johnson had taken me under his wing and taught me the trade when I was a young man. I asked, "What's in it for me?"

"What do you want?"

"We can discuss it over dinner." I'd been looping all afternoon, riding from one end of the subway line to the other, collecting hide along the way, and I was hungry. Even though I had a fat wad of cash tucked in a special pocket hidden inside my jacket that Sean never would have found even if he knew to look for it, I wasn't about to reveal its existence. "Are you hungry?"

Sean nodded.

"Good," I said. "You're paying." I handed him his wallet a second time, and this time I had stripped it of cash.

He stared at me. "How the hell did you do that to me again?"

I smiled. "There's a deli at the corner. They make a good pastrami on rye."

Without waiting to see if Sean would follow, I turned and headed up the block. He matched my stride and held the door open for me when we reached the deli. We ordered, found an empty booth in the back and sat with our sandwiches. The din of the busy deli prevented people around us from easily overhearing anything we might say.

"This is a terrible business to get into," I explained. I was working twice as hard as twenty years earlier just to maintain my lifestyle. "Fewer and fewer people are carrying significant amounts of cash."

"Cash is old-school," Sean said. "I'm after plastic— credit cards, debit cards, gift cards."

"You can turn those?"

"I know a guy."

"We all know a guy," I said. My leg brushed against his under the table. He didn't pull away. "Can you trust yours?"

Sean shrugged. "So far."

His cavalier attitude bothered me. It should have bothered me more, but I was watching him eat—the way he wrapped his lips around the sandwich, the way he took the meat into his mouth, the way he wet his lips with the tip of his tongue between bites—and thoughts that had nothing to do with my profession distracted me. I shifted my leg, rubbing it against his in a way that could seem accidental, but he still didn't pull away. I said, "You need to have a lot of faith in a guy like that. He turns on you and then where will you be?"

"Having my room and board paid by the state."

"That's why I prefer to stick with cash," I said. "Less back-end risk."

Sean leaned forward, "But you have to dip more often than I do," he said, "which exposes you up front."

Above the table we were having a conversation that may have been about fences and risk, but under the table our legs were having a quieter conversation, one that made my cock hard.

We talked—above the table and below—for several more minutes, then finished our sandwiches and stood to go. I dropped some of Sean's money on the table before fanning the young blond. Fanning is the act of lightly touching a pocket to determine if it contains money or a wallet, but I wasn't checking Sean's pockets; I was determining the length, girth and firmness of his erection.

I was impressed and he didn't even know it.

Once we stood on the sidewalk outside the deli, Sean held out his hand and asked, "Do I get my change?"

I ignored both his question and his outstretched hand. I didn't like the idea of taking a stranger to my apartment, but if I wanted him, I had no choice. "Follow me."

My apartment was a third-floor walk-up above a two-story used bookstore three blocks from the deli, and the entrance was a doorway sandwiched between the bookstore and a pawnshop. The building didn't inspire confidence, nor did the stairwell, but my living space occupied the entire top floor, with a large living room, eat-in kitchen, two bedrooms and large bath, all protected by a steel door with a serious deadbolt.

Once inside my apartment, Sean's eyes widened. My ex-boyfriend had decorated the place, and he'd had impeccable taste. He'd also had my bankroll to work with.

"You didn't get all this lifting wallets," Sean said, as I closed and bolted the door.

The young blond standing before me was correct, but I didn't admit it. Over the years I'd lifted many things: jewelry, bearer bonds and other easily fenced valuables, much of it when I was working with Fingers because it often required the work of both a stall and a hitter to walk off with purses, briefcases, courier pouches and other portable containers used to transport valuables. I had been working solo ever since Alzheimer's made Fingers worthless even as a stall, and teaming with my own stall I could again target high-end marks. My cock had grown flaccid during the walk from the deli, but the thought of once again taking down big scores firmed it right up.

I pushed Sean back against the steel door, covered his mouth with mine and shoved my tongue down his throat. I slipped one hand between us and had Sean's belt unfastened, his zipper open and his pants slithering down his thighs before he realized I had my fist wrapped around his cock. I could tell without looking that he'd manscaped his pubic hair into oblivion.

His cock quickly stiffened in my grasp and I pistoned my fist up and down the thick shaft. My weight pinned Sean to the door, and he could barely move his hips forward and back as I fist-fucked him. When he moaned in my mouth, I knew he was about to come, and I quickly covered his cock head with my hand. He came on my palm and when he finished ejaculating, I wiped my hand on his shirt.

We shed clothes as I led Sean down the hall to the master bedroom where I kept a tube of lube and a box of condoms in the dresser drawer. By the time we reached the bedroom, we were both naked and I could appreciate his smooth, young skin; at the same time, I realized that I had not manscaped in months, not since the night Leo realized exactly how I earned my living and declared that he would have no part of it.

Sean didn't seem to care that I'd not groomed. In fact, my mansweater seemed to turn him on in a way that it had never excited my ex. I grabbed the lube and condoms from the dresser, spun Sean around so that he was leaning over the end of the bed, and slathered his ass crack with lube. Then I pulled on a condom and pressed the head of my cock against his slick sphincter. I grabbed his hips and held tight as I pushed forward, easing my cock head into him. Then I drove my shaft deep inside Sean, pulled back and did it again.

I fucked him hard, and I fucked him fast, slamming into the young blond again and again and again until I couldn't hold back any longer. I drove myself into him one last time and then filled the condom with wad after wad of hot ejaculate.

When I finally pulled away, Sean collapsed on the bed. I disposed of the used condom and joined him, holding him in my arms until he unexpectedly fell asleep. Then I eased away from him and, while he slept, went through all his pockets and examined everything in his wallet.

When I finished, I shook him awake. "You have to leave."

"Why?"

"There's supposed to be honor among thieves," I said, "but I don't really know you and I don't trust you. Not yet. Maybe never."

Sean rubbed his eyes and crawled out of bed. He pulled on his clothes, and I walked him to the door. He was about to step onto the landing when he stopped and patted his pockets. He turned back and held out his hand. "My wallet?"

I handed it to him, and he shoved it in his pocket, not even realizing that I'd examined everything in it and that I knew far more about him than he knew about me. He asked, "When will I see you again?"

"Tomorrow morning, early." I told him what time and what subway station. "We'll work the morning rush. I want to watch you dip."

Sean was at the station awaiting my arrival the next morning. He'd already lifted two wallets and he showed me his paltry earnings: thirteen dollars and a stack of credit cards.

"Ditch the plastic," I ordered.

"Why?"

"We're going to spend the morning looping. We get caught with cash it'll be hard to prove where we got it," I explained. "We get caught with plastic there'll be no doubt of its source."

Sean reluctantly discarded the credit cards into the nearest trashcan when we walked past. "What's looping?"

I glanced at my new apprentice. He didn't even know the lingo.

"We're going to ride to the end of the line, then to the other end and then return here," I explained. Some subway lines are only good for morning and evening rush hour during the week, other lines are best on weekends, still others are packed on holidays when out-of-towners visit the city. Over time I would need to teach Sean the differences.

Once aboard, I watched him work the subway train, noted how he picked his marks, and saw how often he failed to come away with anything. At the same time, I was watching Sean I was also dipping, sometimes even lifting wallets from marks he'd been unable to hit. When we stopped for lunch I dissected his technique, from how he selected his marks to his actual handwork.

People near Sean's age are easy marks. Many of them wear earbuds, talk on cell phones, or are wrapped up in some other electronic device and pay no attention to their environment. Unfortunately, they were weaned on plastic and are the least likely to carry cash. The best marks are older people who came of age before the universal acceptance of credit and debit cards, who grew up paying cash and still often do, and who can tell a cashier their change before the cashier can get the answer from the register.

I explained all this to Sean over tuna salad on wheat. He ate a heavier meal despite my observation that it would weigh on his stomach and make him lethargic by midafternoon.

After lunch we returned to the subway, and I taught him how to spot players and the jostling squad—fellow pickpockets and the police—and made him watch me work. He did, indeed, get tired midafternoon, but he also learned fast, and soon I had him working again. During the afternoon I fanned the crotches of a few attractive men, and I copped a good feel of Sean's crotch when we neared our last stop of the day, using a heavy touch so that he knew what was on my mind.

I took him back to my apartment, and we went directly to the master bedroom, where removing our clothes caused only a momentary delay. Sean dropped to his knees in front of me, cupped my heavy ball sac in one hand and held my stiff shaft with his other hand as he leaned forward and took the swollen mushroom cap between his lips. He painted my cock head with his tongue and then slowly took my entire length into his mouth. As soon as I felt his warm breath against the dark tangle of my crotch hair, he pulled all the way back until his teeth caught on my glans.

He did it again and again, kneading my balls at the same time. Sean's oral skills were like his pickpocketing skills—they were effective but lacked finesse—and soon I wrapped my fingers in his short silky hair and held his head as I began pulling my hips back and pushing forward, meeting his descending face with each of my thrusts.

When it became obvious I was about to come, Sean squeezed my balls together and I slammed into his face one last time, spewing thick wads of hot ejaculate against the back of his throat. He held my rapidly deflating cock in his mouth until it stopped spasming, and then he pushed himself to his feet.

I wasn't completely satisfied, and my cock rapidly regained its former stature. I grabbed the lube and condoms from my dresser drawer, spun Sean around and took him from behind, just as I had the previous day. This time, though, Sean's cock was hard when I entered him. As I pounded into his ass, he took his own cock in his fist and beat a staccato rhythm in opposition to the steady pounding he was receiving from behind.

He came first, spewing ejaculate across my carpet, and then I came, filling the condom and holding his ass tight against my crotch until I could easily pull away. I discarded the come-filled condom and then we fell across the bed together.

We talked about the things Sean had learned that day, and we talked about the things he had yet to learn. He was eager, undisciplined and lacked the gift to be a truly great hitter. But he could develop into an excellent stall, a great lay and a partner in all things.

I looked into his pale blue eyes and smiled.

There's so much I can teach Sean, in the subway and in the bedroom, and I know we have a lifetime of adventures ahead of us.

STAND BY YOUR MAN

My client had been practicing Tai Chi before I interrupted him, and he wore only white gauze pants—loose, comfortable, and so diaphanous in the hot Texas sun that I knew he wore nothing beneath them. His smoothly shaved chest glistened with a perspiration sheen and his muscles flowed under his sun-bronzed skin with a fluid grace as he closed the distance between us.

Jeremy carried two tumblers half full of Jack rocks, placed one on the patio table before me, and settled into the chair opposite mine. Then he leaned forward. Piercing blue eyes captured my attention, just as they had the day we'd first met in my office downtown. He wore his wheat-blond hair long, parted in the center, and tucked behind his ears. A lock of hair slipped from behind his left ear and curled around the corner of his mouth, like a close parenthesis to the sensual expression of his full lips.

"He doesn't love me anymore," my client said. "I'm not sure he ever did."

I sipped from my tumbler, the Jack burning its way down the back of my throat. "Do you love him?"

Jeremy looked away, his gaze taking in the neatly manicured lawn, the blooming bluebonnets growing along the back fence, and the new Lexus parked in the rear drive. He returned his attention to me, wet his lips with the tip of his tongue, and said, "I love this."

I felt my body react to my client's presence, the crotch of my pants growing uncomfortably tight, sweat beading on my upper lip, and my pulse quickening. I took another sip from the tumbler. The ice had nearly melted and the Jack felt warm in my throat, warmer still when it reached the pit of my stomach. I hadn't eaten since the previous night, and then only a bean burrito I had leftover from the day before.

My client watched my face and waited.

I reached into my briefcase and retrieved a manila envelope containing a dozen color photographs. I slid the envelope across the table to my client. He turned it over and worried at the brass clasp until one of the arms separated from it.

"I came for my master's," he said. As he spoke, he worried at the remaining arm of the envelope's brass clasp. "I worked as his graduate assistant, grading papers and researching obscure references in Hemingway's short stories."

My .38 felt heavy under my left arm, the thick leather of the holster ironing my shirt to my ribs. I considered removing my jacket but didn't. Instead, I finished my Jack.

"One evening, after a Christmas party at the dean's house, his car wouldn't start. He asked me to carry him home, and when I did, he invited me inside for a nightcap." Jeremy pushed the stray lock of hair behind his ear, wet his lips a second time, and continued. "I knew what he wanted. I wanted it just as much as he did."

My client leaned across the table and touched the back of my hand with the tips of his fingers. An electric tingle shot through my body, and my balls tightened. "You know what that's like, don't you, to want someone so bad you don't care about the consequences?"

"Yeah," I said. My throat felt parched, and I wished I hadn't finished my drink. I subtly shifted position to relieve the pressure at my crotch, but I didn't move my hand. "I know what that's like."

"I finished the semester, then moved in. I never went back to school, never—" He didn't finish the sentence and we stared deep into each other's eyes for a full minute before my client pulled his hand away. "How much do I owe you?"

I named a figure.

"That's what it comes down to, then, isn't it?" He leaned back in his seat. "A few thousand dollars... infidelity..."

I returned to my office with half a dozen crisp, new Benjamins tucked into my money clip, and a still-painful tightening in my crotch. I knew better than to become involved with the people who kept me in business, but I couldn't deny the physical reaction I had to my client's presence.

I'd felt it that first time, when I'd been sitting behind

my desk, thumbing through a stack of unopened mail. He'd knocked on my door and then pushed into my office without waiting for my response. He dressed well, but simply: form-fitting teal polo shirt over crisply pressed khaki pants and highly polished penny loafers without socks. Unlike the hulking muscles I'd developed wrestling bail jumpers and repossessing cars from irate owners delinquent on payments, he had the sculpted look of a young man who exercised as if his body were a work of art. If we had met in a bar, I would have offered him a drink, or two. Instead, he hired me to follow the man he lived with, a tenured English professor at the university.

As we concluded our business, and a retainer consisting of enough dead presidents to pay my outstanding debts had moved from his wallet to my desk drawer, my client had stood and offered me his hand. I stood, and when I took his hand in mine, he smiled and wet his lips with the tip of his tongue. Then he thanked me, and a moment later I found myself alone in my office, the tightening at my crotch so painful that I considered relieving the pressure myself.

I felt that way now as I listened to the messages on my answering machine. I returned a call from a woman who thought her neighbor was poisoning her cat, and I talked her out of hiring a private detective by convincing her to keep her pussy inside. Then I returned a call from an Austin-based insurance company that occasionally subcontracted insurance fraud cases to me. They hired me to investigate a worker's comp claimant who insisted he'd hurt his back moving a skid of paper at a local printing company. I finished my workday by closing my client's case, marking the account as paid in full, and stuffing my notes into a battered black filing cabinet where old cases usually disappear forever.

When I arrived home, I hung my suit and my shoulder holster on the back of my bedroom door, and I changed into sweatpants. As soon as I felt comfortable, I sat in my living room and ate Chinese takeout while watching the six o'clock news. Near the end of the program, a familiar English professor discussed his latest book, yet another examination of Hemingway's code hero. Beside him during the entire interview sat his current graduate assistant, a dark-haired young man not unlike Jeremy. I watched mind-numbing sitcoms for the rest of the evening, finally turning in halfway through the ten o'clock news.

An insistent pounding woke me some time after midnight. I retrieved my .38, thumbed back the hammer, and crept down the dark hallway wearing only my boxers. I opened the front door and found Jeremy standing on the porch, reeking of alcohol, a nearly empty bottle of Jack Daniel's tightly gripped in one fist. I stared at him through the screen. "Why are you here?"

He raised the bottle to his lips and drained it before answering. "He kicked me out. I didn't have any place else to go."

"How did you find me?"

"How hard can it be?" he said. "You're in the phone book."

My boxers began to tent as I stared at him. "Go to a hotel."

"And do what?" he asked. "Sleep in the lobby? I don't have any money. I never had any money. Everything I had belonged to him, and he took it all before he kicked me out."

I pointed my chin at the Lexus parked at the curb. "And that?"

He spun around to look at the car, lost his balance and nearly fell off the top step. He caught himself against the wrought-iron railing, then threw the empty Jack Daniel's bottle at the car. When it fell short and shattered on the sidewalk, he turned back to me and smiled. "He doesn't know I took it."

I uncocked my revolver, then unlatched my screen door and pushed it open. "Get in here before the neighbors call the cops."

Jeremy stepped past me and into my living room. He stood close enough I could feel the heat from his body, and I could smell his sweat and his aftershave through the stench of alcohol. I thought I detected a hint of copper and sulphur underneath it all.

He turned once inside, saw my .38 for the first time, and wet his lips. "I like your gun."

I offered him the spare room, showed him where I kept my towels if he wanted to shower, and returned to my bedroom. I slipped the .38 into my holster, then slid between the cool sheets and closed my eyes.

When I felt weight on the far side of my mattress, I opened my eyes to find Jeremy beside me. He had showered and he smelled of Irish Spring and baby powder. He was completely sober.

"Hold me," he whispered. "I don't want to be alone."

I felt the familiar tightening at my crotch as he snuggled into my arms and curled against me. He toyed with the hair on my chest, one finger drawing invisible designs as his hand moved lower, over my taut abdomen and under the waistband of my boxers.

I turned then, and took Jeremy's head in my hands, his still-damp blond hair threading through my fingers, and I covered his mouth with mine. His lips were full, soft, and moist, and he kept his eyes open as I thrust my tongue between them. Our kiss was long, and deep, and hard, and it took my breath away.

When it finally ended, I whispered in the dark, "I've wanted to do that since the day you walked into my office."

Jeremy placed a finger on my lips, silencing me. He pushed the sheet aside and slid down the bed. I lifted my hips when he tugged at my boxers. A moment later they lay on the floor and my client's warm breath tickled the dark thatch of hair at the juncture of my thighs.

I knew I shouldn't let desire override common sense. I knew I shouldn't become involved with a client, not even with a former client, but in that place, at that time, I wasn't thinking. I wasn't thinking and I should have been.

Months had passed since the end of my last relationship and I had let myself go, failing to perform even rudimentary personal grooming. My hirsute condition didn't deter my client, though. He took my hairy balls into his mouth, one at a time and then both together.

By then, my cock had grown painfully erect. Jeremy released his oral grip on my balls and used the tip of his tongue to draw a wet line from my ball sac up the underside of my shaft. He took my spongy soft cock head in his mouth and hooked his teeth behind my glans.

As his tongue painted my glans with his saliva, he cupped my scrotum in one hand and massaged my testicles. Using the tip of his middle finger, he stroked the sensitive spot behind my ball sac. I thought I would explode in his mouth right then, but I didn't.

Instead, I reached down and wrapped my fingers in his hair, pushing against the back of his head and urging him to take the entire length of my shaft into his mouth. I closed my eyes as he took my shaft in slowly and then drew back until just my cock head remained between his lips. Then he did it again.

Saliva dripped trickled down my scrotum, wetting the hand Jeremy was using to massage my sac. The third time he lowered his face into my lap, he pressed one saliva-slick finger against the tight pucker of my ass and drove it into me.

My eyes snapped open.

He massaged my prostate with his finger as he continued face fucking me, and I could not restrain myself. I came, and came hard, firing a thick wad of hot spunk against the back of Jeremy's throat.

He swallowed every drop and didn't release his oral grip on my cock until it stopped throbbing in his mouth.

I wasn't finished with him, though. I wanted more. Much more. And my cock quickly responded.

I rolled over and reached into the drawer of my nightstand. I retrieved a tube of lube, squeezed a drop of lubricant onto my middle finger, and applied it to my client's tightly puckered sphincter.

He rose up on his knees and grabbed the headboard as I positioned myself behind him and grabbed his slim hips. I pressed the head of my cock against Jeremy's lubricated hole and pressed forward until I buried my entire length within him. Then I drew back and pushed forward.

I held Jeremy's hips as I fucked him, driving into him again and again.

He reached back, took my right hand in his, and guided it to his erection. Then he wrapped my fingers around his shaft, and I didn't need any additional encouragement.

As I fucked his ass, I pistoned my hand up and down Jeremy's cock shaft.

He came first, spewing come on the sheets, and then I came, firing my second wad deep inside him.

When we finally tired of one another, we shifted position, trying to get comfortable on the wet sheets. When we finally settled ourselves, we were spooned together, facing the back of the now-closed bedroom door, his smooth rear end pressed against my crotch. I held Jeremy, my breath tickling the hair behind his ear, and I fell asleep.

I woke the next morning to find myself alone, my bedroom rank with the stale scent of our sex. I pushed myself out of bed and padded to the bathroom.

Jeremy had left it a disaster, the tile floor covered with rust-stained towels still damp from the night before. I snatched one up, examined the stains closely and recognized blood. Under the towels, my client had left his whiskey-soaked clothing.

I showered quickly, pulled on my clothes, and grabbed my empty shoulder holster. My client, a pair of jeans, a T-shirt, and my .38 had disappeared.

I could think of only one place to go. I drove to the English professor's house and found it surrounded by police. I talked my way inside.

A shotgun blast had removed the back of the professor's head and had spread it across the bedroom wall. Two detectives showed me the body.

"Looks like suicide," said one of the detectives. We had known each other for years, our paths crossing more often than either of us cared to admit. "Hell of a time to kill himself, though, what with the new book and all."

"But these pretty much tell the story," said the other detective. He indicated a dozen color photographs of the English professor's current graduate assistant taking his oral exams from the professor. The photos had been scattered about the room.

"One thing bothers me, though," said the first detective. "If he killed himself, wouldn't blood be on top of the photographs, not under them?"

The second detective looked closer. "Someone threw these here after he died."

They both looked at me. I told them about Jeremy, about how he'd hired me, how I'd taken the photos of the dead professor, and how my client had spent the night in my house. I didn't tell the detectives what we'd done all night, letting them believe my client had slept in my spare bedroom.

And I told them about my missing .38.

With nothing left to tell, I promised I'd make a formal statement whenever the detectives were ready, and then I drove to my office.

I'd barely unlocked the door when the phone rang.

I recognized Jeremy's voice immediately and told him about the scene at his home.

"It's not my home anymore," he said. "Home is where the heart is, and there hasn't been any heart there in a long time."

"You used me last night."

"We used each other," he said. "I needed you and you wanted me, wanted me so bad you didn't care about the consequences."

I swallowed hard, and then asked, "What now?"

"When you live in a world without hope," he said,

"you try to find a reason to go on. Last night, with you, just delayed the inevitable."

He disconnected the line and I sat with the phone pressed against my ear, listening to the buzz.

A week later, two college students found the ass end of Jeremy's Lexus jutting out of the river just south of campus. When the police arrived, they discovered his body inside the car, one hand still gripping my .38, and a slug from my .38 embedded in the roof of the car. It had first traveled through the roof of his mouth and out the back of his head.

Police closed both cases promptly, the university encouraged a graduate student in the English department to seek educational opportunities elsewhere, and, between visits to the police department, I exposed the false claims of the worker's comp claimant.

During the many months since then, when I sit in my darkened living room and my only company is a few fingers of Jack, I think about the consequences of desire and about cases that should remain closed.

MAC AND CHEESE GET BOXED

Mac and I had inside information and knew that Darby Winchester's sleep disorder required absolute blackness. We had thought the absence of light would work to our advantage, and we studied photographs and cell phone video of his bedroom until we knew the layout better than we knew our own sleeping quarters.

Around two a.m. on a night our inside source assured us we would find Winchester home alone, we entered his two-story Tudor through an unlocked kitchen door, hustled up the back stairs, and found his bedroom easily enough. Mac pushed open the door and I reached Winchester's bedside in two long strides.

I retrieved a plastic Ziploc bag from my pocket, pulled from it a rag doused with ether, and slapped the rag over our target's face before he could wake enough to notice our presence in the room.

After I returned the rag to the Ziploc bag and the bag to my pocket, I slapped a strip of duct tape over the man's mouth. I tied his ankles together while Mac tied his hands behind his back, and then I pulled a pillowcase over his head. After we rolled him up in the bed linens like a human burrito, I hoisted Winchester over my shoulder and carried him down the back stairs to the florist's van Mac had boosted two hours earlier.

A few minutes later, Mac eased the van down the alley, and we pulled off our black ski masks.

"That was easy enough, Cheese," Mac said. Because I was from Wisconsin and the Chicago crew didn't like guys from Wisconsin, my name had morphed from Charles to Cheesehead and then morphed again to Cheese after I paired up with Mac and some ass hole realized how well Mac and Cheese went together. "Everything went according to plan."

"Just drive," I told my partner. Enough of our jobs had gone south on us that I didn't like to jinx things by patting ourselves on the back too soon.

Manny the Torch had brought this opportunity to our attention. Anthony "The Ant" Piscatolli had provided seed money and established our alibi for the night. In exchange for the tip, Manny would collect a finder's fee, and for his seal of approval The Ant would receive a healthy cut of the half million we expected to gross. We had disappointed The Ant with a previous job—a jewelry store heist that netted us a bag of paste and a parking ticket—and had assured him that this job would put us back in his good graces. We were surprised when he agreed to back our play.

Neither of spoke again until we reached the abandoned warehouse we had scoped out the previous week. As Mac pulled in, the van's headlights revealed a worktable pushed against an inside wall, a spool of wire, and several broken pallets nearby. After he cut the engine and lights, moonlight through broken windows illuminated the inside of the warehouse, providing more than enough light for what we were doing. I pulled the human burrito from the back of the van, unrolled him, and sat him naked on the concrete floor with his back against an inside wall.

I motioned to Mac, and we pulled our ski masks down before I jerked the pillowcase off the head of the man we'd abducted.

My eyes widened in surprise. "Who the fuck are you?"

We'd bagged the wrong guy. He said, "Murph."

I couldn't tell if that was his name or just the only sound he could push through the duct tape covering his mouth. I jerked off the tape.

"Okay, Murph," I said. "What were you doing in Winchester's bed?"

"Sleeping."

"Where's Winchester?"

"Fuck if I know." Murph's blue eyes glared up at me. "Winchester's cell phone rang around midnight. He only talked for a few seconds. After he hung up, he pulled on his clothes and told me to fix myself breakfast and let myself out in the morning. Then he grabbed a suit bag and left."

"He done that before?"

"Never," Murph said. "He usually kicked me out at sunrise."

I stared at the naked blond sitting trussed up on the

floor in front of me. He was younger than Winchester by at least forty years, had a sculpted body that indicated a regular workout routine, and had manscaped in a way that suggested he was accustomed to other men staring at him, just like Mac and I were staring at him.

Mac elbowed me. "What do we do with him?"

Murph eyed our crotches. "Couple of big bucks like you should be able to think of something."

"He's kind of cute," Mac said. "We could hump him and dump him."

I turned to my partner. He thought with his secondary head more often that he thought with his primary head, and I could tell from the bulge in his pants that the naked manflesh in front of us was affecting him as much as it was affecting me. I said, "We need to consider our options."

"You think," Mac said. "I'm getting a piece of this."

He stripped off his jacket and I saw the shoulder holster and the .38 that had been concealed beneath it.

Incredulous, I asked, "You brought a gun?"

"If we'd had one last time," he said as he laid his jacket and shoulder holster on one end of the worktable, "we could have shot the old codger behind the counter before he could reach for the shotgun."

"And you might have gotten us both killed," I said. As it was, we'd seen what the old man had in his hands and had scrambled out of the place before he'd pulled the trigger and blown the glass out of the door.

Mac stripped off the rest of his clothes, leaving on only his black ski mask. He was the physical opposite of the young man we'd abducted, built like a refrigerator box with a dark man-jacket already threaded with silver. He thrust his erect cock in the young man's face. "If you can do the old man, you can do me."

Murph glanced at me. Then he sat up straight and took the head of Mac's cock between his lips.

"Take it all." Mac grabbed the back of Murph's head and thrust the full length of his hard cock into Murph's oral cavity. He pulled back and thrust forward again and again, his heavy ball sac bouncing against the young man's chin as he face-fucked Murph.

I couldn't help myself. I watched every stroke. And I knew from experience that when Mac suddenly stiffened, he had just shot his wad into Murph's mouth.

He held Murph's head for a moment longer, then backed away. A thread of come connected the two men until Murph turned his head and spat a thick wad of spunk onto the concrete floor.

"That the best you got?" he asked Mac. Then he turned his attention on me. "What about you?"

"He doesn't do strange," Mac said. He hooked his hand under Murph's arm, lifted him to his feet, and bent him over the worktable. He approached from behind and ran his saliva-slickened cock up and down the man's ass crack. Then he stopped.

"This isn't going to work," he told me. "I've got to untie his feet so I can spread his legs."

Maybe I should have stopped my partner, but I didn't. I let Mac untie Murph's legs and spread them wide apart. By then his cock was again fully erect and he pressed his cock head against the young man's ass pucker. He grabbed Murph's hips and drove his cock inside the younger man. Murph's hands were still tied behind his back, and they were trapped against Mac's belly as Mac leaned into the younger man and pumped in and out of his ass.

"You can do better than that, can't you?" Murph taunted. "Even Winchester did better with his old dick."

Mac slammed into him harder and faster, causing the worktable to slam against the wall with a staccato rhythm.

When Mac came, he came hard, driving into Murph one last time, and he stood with his crotch pressed against Murph's ass until his cock finally softened and he could pull away easily.

I didn't want any strange, but watching Mac bang the younger man had given me a throbbing erection, causing my chinos to tent. Mac noticed.

He stepped up close to me, unzipped my pants, and unthreaded my cock from the confining cotton of my tightie-whities. He wrapped one fist around my stiff shaft and pumped his fist up and down.

"I knew you would enjoy watching," he whispered. His warm breath tickled my ear. He unfastened my chinos and they dropped to my ankles. "You always do."

He dropped to his knees and, with my cock still jutting from my underwear, wrapped his lips around the swollen head. He painted my cock head with his tongue and then took the first inch of my shaft into his mouth. He pulled his face back and then pushed forward.

As his head bobbed forward and back, taking a little more of me into his mouth each time, Mac reached through the leg hole of my tighty-whities and grabbed my heavy ball sac. As he kneaded my nuts together, his head continued bobbing up and down my shaft.

Soon I couldn't hold back any longer. I grabbed the back of his head and fuck-fucked my partner. While Mac blew me, we lost track of the man we'd accidentally abducted, and just as my wad exploded against the back of Mac's throat, I felt something against the base of my skull and heard a sound that made my dick shrivel—the sound of a revolver being cocked.

I turned my head and saw Murph standing naked behind me, his cock stiff as a steel beam. He had freed his hands, had picked up Mac's .38, and now had the upper hand. Mac was busy swallowing my load and didn't notice the power shift inside the warehouse.

"Get up, Mac," I said.

"Yeah, get up Mac," Murph commanded.

As soon as my partner saw the situation we were in, his dick shriveled as small as mine.

Murph made Mac tie my hands behind my back using the rope that had tied his hands. Then he cold-cocked my partner with the butt of the revolver. He rolled Mac onto his stomach and tied his wrists together with the rope from his ankles. Then he checked the job Mac had done tying my wrists together, ensuring that my partner had done a better job tying me up than he had done with Murph. He found the spool of electrical wire, sat us back-to-back, and wrapped the wire around us a few dozen times, his erect cock bobbing in front of my face each time he circled us.

After we were securely bound, Murph pulled off our ski masks and threw them aside.

"Didn't want any strange, huh?" Murph asked as he stood in front of me. He held the revolver in one hand and his cock in the other, and jerked himself off until he came on my face.

"Winchester set this all up," he said. "He figured you two morons would dump my body by the side of the road and he'd be rid of me forever. The guy who called him last night had to be in on it, too, some guy he called Mr. Ant. Well, they aren't getting off that easy."

Murph pulled on Mac's oversized clothes and drove away in the stolen florist's van, leaving me to watch the sunrise through the broken windows. Even though I was mostly dressed, with my chinos still tangled around my ankles, I was better off than Mac, who was completely naked without his ski mask.

I had a lot of time to think before Mac finally came to, and I told him what he had missed. I couldn't figure out the connection between Darby Winchester and Antonio "The Ant" Piscatolli, but The Ant had set us up to fail. We had fucked up the job we had thought we were doing by abducting the wrong man and we had fucked up the job we had been set up to do by letting him escape. Whether Murph got his revenge against Winchester didn't matter. The Ant would not forgive our failure.

Mac listened carefully to everything I told him and then, after a moment of silence while it all sank in, asked, "Now what, Cheese?"

"If we get out of this alive," I told him. "We might want to move south and get into another line of work."

TIDES

Jamie and I were the only people on the white-sand beach, and we didn't notice the lone swimmer until he walked out of the Caribbean wearing nothing at all.

My cock stirred at the sight, and I blinked. Twice.

Jamie nudged me. "Do you see what I see?"

"So, I'm not imagining it?"

"If you are," he said, "then I'm having the same fantasy."

The sun-bronzed swimmer finger-combed his long black hair away from his face. The motion of his powerful arms made his broad chest expand and his already-tight abdomen constrict. His thick, uncut phallus and heavy scrotum hung from a dark nest between his thighs, and there was no evidence at all that the warm Caribbean water had caused shrinkage. I had never in my life seen a man so perfect.

"They didn't say anything about *this* in the brochure," Jamie said. "I think there would be more men on this beach if they had."

We had come to the island during spring break to get

away from the repressive Baptist university where we were enrolled as sophomores and had booked ourselves into a little-known, out-of-the way place with few of the amenities the expensive resorts on the far side of the island offered. The best things our two-room cottage had going for it were the secluded white-sand beach, the sea view and the privacy that would allow us the opportunity to explore each other at leisure. The trip was Jamie's idea and he'd paid for everything. He thought it would be good for our relationship to get away from the university.

Jamie and I couldn't take our eyes off the naked swimmer, though, and we watched as he walked north along the shoreline until he disappeared. As if in a daze, the swimmer never acknowledged us nor ever acted as if he knew we were present.

I leaned over. "If my cock was any harder," I whispered in Jamie's ear, "I could pound nails with it."

"Do you want to go back to the cottage?"

Of course, I did, and it wasn't long before we stripped off our flip-flops and board shorts.

Jamie and I have been together since the day we met during freshman orientation, one blond gravitating toward another with the knowledge that we shared something our classmates didn't—something that would likely get us expelled if it became common knowledge—and during the eighteen months or so we had been together we had discovered each other's likes and dislikes.

As soon as we had stripped off our board shorts and tank tops, I sat on the side of the bed and Jamie knelt between my widespread thighs. He cupped my balls in his hand and took the swollen head of my cock in his mouth. He spanked it with his tongue and then licked away the pre-come that oozed from the pee slit. As he kneaded my nuts together, he slowly took more of my cock into his mouth until he had swallowed about two-thirds of it. Then he drew his mouth back until his pearly white teeth caught on the spongy soft ridge of my glans. He did it again and again, covering my shaft with his saliva, never quite taking all of me down his throat.

Jamie wrapped his free hand around his erect cock and began tugging at it, jerking off as fast as he could. All the while he continued his oral assault on my erection. Jamie came first—he usually does—spewing spunk on my shin, the bedspread and the carpet. By then I was nearing release. I grabbed the back of Jamie's head, threading my fingers through his short, blond hair and pulling his head down as I thrust my hips upward, slapping his chin with my balls and sinking my cock so deep it triggered his gag reflex.

I came hard, firing hot spunk against the back of Jamie's throat as I released my grip on his head, allowing him to pull back so that he could swallow every drop of my come.

After he had swallowed and had licked my cock clean, Jamie rose from the floor and settled onto the bed next to me. "Seeing that guy come out of the water really turned you on, didn't it?"

I had been with other guys before Jamie, and I had been with other guys since meeting Jamie—though he didn't know about any of them—and I knew I had to tread carefully. "He was nice to look at," I admitted, "but he isn't you."

Jamie and I saw the swimmer later that evening when we went to a beachside bar a mile from our hotel, a place that was little more than a roof with corner supports, a bar at one end and a dozen tables at the other. He had dressed in a floral print shirt, khaki shorts and leather sandals, but it was difficult to look at him without remembering all the sun-bronzed skin we had seen earlier that afternoon. He sat alone, drinking shot after shot of whiskey as he stared out at the water.

Jamie and I sat at the bar nursing piña coladas, sharing funny stories about our past that wouldn't have been funny if we had been sober and swapping spit every so often, not caring one whit what our bar mates—mostly locals—thought about our public display of affection. Even though I was with Jamie, I kept glancing at the swimmer. Finally, after enough drinks had given me the courage, I pushed myself off the bar stool and made my way to where he sat.

"Hey," I said.

He looked up and I realized he had at least fifteen years on us.

"We saw you this afternoon." I indicated Jamie, who was gripping the bar tightly to keep from falling off his stool. "On the beach."

He said nothing.

"Hob lay gringo?" I slurred. "Polly voo American?"

"I speak English." He had a deep voice, like Darth Vader without the respirator.

"We saw you drinking alone," I continued. "We thought you might like company."

The swimmer glanced at Jamie and then returned his attention to me. He kicked the chair across from him out from under the table and it slid backward a good three feet. "So sit."

As I sat, I motioned for Jamie. He staggered over with our drinks and dropped onto the chair to my left.

"I'm Kyle," I said. "This is Jamie."

The swimmer saw that our glasses were nearly empty, so he caught the heavyset waitress's attention and indicated with a circular wave of his index finger that he wanted a round of drinks. She waddled away.

Because the swimmer had yet to introduce himself, I asked, "And you are?"

He stared at his empty shot glass for a moment and then said, "Jack. Just call me Jack."

I said, "Good thing you aren't drinking Shirley Temples."

Jamie giggled. He'd matched me drink for drink, but he couldn't handle his liquor.

When the waitress returned, Jamie reached for his wallet because he always paid when we were together. He had a trust fund, and I only had a Pell grant. Jack put one hand on Jamie's forearm and stopped him. To the waitress, he said, "Put it on my tab."

She nodded and moved on to the next table.

"Thanks, Jack," I said.

He held his shot glass up in a silent toast, so we lifted our piña coladas. Then the three of us drank. Jamie almost poked his eye out with the red plastic sword holding his maraschino cherry and pineapple wedge together. I sucked from my straw. Jack emptied his shot glass and returned it to the tabletop. "Why are you two here?"

"Because it's the only bar for miles," Jamie slurred.

"It's spring break," I explained, "and we didn't want to go where everybody else went. Why are you here?"

He stared over my shoulder, perhaps looking at the sea again, before answering. "I'm waiting."

"For what?" I asked.

"For the tide to turn," he replied. He was silent for a moment, and then he said, "You ask a lot of questions."

I jerked a thumb at myself. "Journalism major."

"And your friend?"

Jamie had one arm on the table and was resting his forehead on it.

"Undeclared," I said.

"Five-year plan?"

"If he's lucky." Jamie was killing time until he inherited his grandfather's money, and college was just as good a way to do it as any other. I finished my drink and reached for Jamie's.

"Looks like your friend's ready to go back to your room," Jack said.

"I think we both are."

Jack had the waitress bring him an unopened bottle of whiskey. Then he helped me hoist Jamie to his feet and walk him to the exit, which wasn't anything more than a step down from a raised floor to a gravel parking lot.

"How'd you get here?"

"Walked."

"Your friend's in no condition to walk back," Jack said. "Let me give you a ride."

We carried Jamie to Jack's rental car, poured him into the backseat, and then I joined Jack in the front. I watched as he drove, and he watched the road. There were no streetlights to illuminate the two-lane highway, only the soft glow of a quarter moon filtering through the overhanging trees and the rental car's headlights slicing through the darkness ahead of us. Jack drove attentively, like a man who didn't think he would pass a sobriety test if he were pulled over.

When we reached our rental cottage, Jack helped me get Jamie to the bedroom and we dropped him across the king-size bed.

"Are you staying here?" I asked. *Here* was six two-room cottages and a building containing the office and a kitchen that served a buffet breakfast and nothing else. We hadn't seen a maid the entire time we'd been there.

"No," Jack said. "I have a house farther down the beach." He told me which one. I'd seen it from the road on our ride from the airport. It wasn't a house; it was a villa.

"You have that entire place to yourself?"

Jack smiled wanly. "I do now."

I had no idea what the hell he meant, but I wasn't sober enough to pursue the conversation. Feeling dizzy, I steadied myself by grabbing his upper arm. Even wasted I appreciated the firm muscle I had wrapped my fingers around, and my cock stirred in my board shorts.

"You're a good-looking guy," I slurred.

Jack peeled my fingers from his arm and encouraged me to lie on the bed next to Jamie. When I did, I passed out.

I awoke the next morning to the sound of Jamie violently expelling the contents of his stomach. I pressed pillows to my ears, but I couldn't completely block the sound. When I heard the shower, I climbed from bed and pulled on clean board shorts, a tank top, and my flip-flops. I left Jamie in the cottage and walked north along the beach until I came to steps carved into the face of a cliff that led up to the villa Jack was renting.

The villa's wide stone porch had a waist-high retaining wall on the cliff side and, after I climbed high enough to see over it, I found Jack sitting at a glass-topped table, nursing a cup of coffee. He'd seen me coming and had an empty cup waiting on the far side of the table. After I sat, he filled it from a silver pitcher and asked, "Why are you here?"

"Isn't it obvious?"

"You want to seduce me."

I didn't confirm or deny his supposition. Instead, I lifted the coffee cup to my lips and sipped.

"Do you always get what you want?" he asked.

"Usually," I replied. "Do you?"

"I do," he said, "but I can't always hold on to it."

He went inside and returned with a framed photograph of a slim blond with model good looks. "I thought Randal was the one," Jack said. "He didn't feel the same about me."

"What happened?"

"A relationship is like the tide. It ebbs and it flows. Right now, the tide is out, but he'll be back." Jack paused and looked out at the sea. "I just don't know when."

I finished my coffee, thanked him and returned the way I had come.

Jamie had showered and dressed and was standing in front of the bathroom mirror fixing his hair. "Where've you been?"

"I went for coffee."

He glanced at my reflection in the mirror. "And you didn't bring any back?"

"I didn't eat," I said. "I thought you might want breakfast."

He did.

We spent that day exploring the island and we spent that night exploring each other. As we lay in bed afterward, Jamie asked, "You were thinking about him, weren't you?"

I turned and looked a question at him.

"You know who I mean," he said. "The swimmer."

I didn't deny it. "Why do you ask?"

"You didn't make love to me," he said. "You *fucked* me."

Jamie turned away and fell asleep with his back to me.

I stared at the ceiling for the longest time, certain that this trip would not turn out the way Jamie had wanted it to.

Friday afternoon we crossed paths with Jack at a little restaurant in town. Jamie and I were sitting at a table outside, eating conch fritters and French fries, when Jack came walking down the street.

He saw us and stopped at our table. "Your week's almost up, isn't it, boys?"

"We leave tomorrow morning," I told him.

He turned his attention to me. "Not much time left," he said. "Did you get everything you wanted?"

"Not yet."

After Jack walked away, Jamie leaned across the table and grabbed my forearm. "What the *hell* was that all about?"

I made a dismissive gesture with my free hand. "It's nothing."

But it wasn't. That evening I took Jamie out drinking and made certain he downed two or three piña coladas to every one of mine. Then I hired a cab to return us to the cottage and paid the driver extra to help me manhandle Jamie into the bedroom.

After I was certain he was settled, I changed clothes and slipped out of the cottage.

Jack had watched me walking up the beach and he met me

on the back porch of his villa. He wore a blue silk robe and held two shots of whiskey. He handed one to me.

When he held his shot glass up, I touched the rim of my glass to his. Then we knocked them back.

I'd never had whiskey straight—I'd always had it mixed with diet Coke—and it made my throat burn and my eyes water.

"Man's drink," Jack said.

I didn't argue. Was I now a man?

We put our empty shot glasses on the retaining wall.

"You're leaving tomorrow."

I nodded.

"And you've come to make one last pass at me."

I wanted him. I had wanted him from the moment he walked out of the sea. I wet my lips and nodded.

There was no need to seduce him and no need for foreplay. We both knew what we wanted. Jack undid the sash and his robe fell open to reveal a thick, uncut phallus and the wild nest of black hair it sprouted from. I dropped to my knees, wrapped one hand around his rapidly rising cock and pulled back his foreskin to reveal the swollen purple head.

I took his cock in my mouth, hooked my teeth behind the glans and painted his cock head with my tongue, soaking it with saliva. Then I slowly took his entire length into my mouth before I drew back. I did that twice more before Jack grabbed my head and face-fucked me. His heavy sac slapped against my chin each time he buried his cock in my mouth. When his sac began to tighten and his breath began to catch, I knew he was about to come. I prepared myself for the geyser.

He came, firing thick wads of hot spunk against the back of my throat. I tried hard to swallow it all, but I couldn't. Some of it leaked out and dripped to the stone porch at my knees.

When his thick cock stopped spasming, he pulled away, took my hand, and pulled me to my feet. Then he shoved one hand into the waistband of my board shorts and pulled me close. He unfastened my shorts and they dropped to my feet. I wasn't wearing anything beneath them, and my cock was already hard.

I peeled off my tank top, stepped out of my shorts, and kicked off my flip-flops. Then he spun me around and bent me over the waist-high rock retaining wall so that I was facing the sea.

So that he was facing the sea.

He wet his middle finger and pressed the tip against the tight pucker of my ass. Before I could ask if he had lube, Jack buried his finger to the second knuckle.

I slowly opened to him, but he was impatient. A moment later I felt the spongy head of his cock press against my ass, surprised at how quickly he had gotten a second erection. He eased his cock head past my sphincter and, once it was in me, grabbed my hips and thrust hard, burying his cock deep inside me.

My arm flailed out, knocking one of the shot glasses off the retaining wall. It shattered somewhere below.

Jack held me tight as he drew back and pushed forward. I braced myself against the wall with one hand

and used the other to grab my own cock, pumping the engorged shaft in counter rhythm to Jack's powerful thrusts.

I came first, spewing come across the rock wall.

Then Jack came again, firing a thick wad deep inside my ass. His body trembled as he held me pinned against the retaining wall, and neither of us moved until his cock softened enough to slip free.

Without a word, he took my hand and led me into the villa, up the stairs and into the master bedroom, a room big enough to play half-court basketball in, filled with heavy, oversized furniture. The French doors had been flung open for an unimpeded view of the Caribbean, and a light breeze tickled the curtains.

I excused myself to use the bathroom and, while washing my hands afterward, discovered a pair of toothbrushes in a cup and two different colognes on the counter next to the sink. Jack had not come to the island alone. I returned to the bedroom where Jack stood next to the open French doors, staring out.

"Where did Randal go, Jack?"

He turned. "Swimming."

"Alone?"

"No."

Before I could ask another question, Jack pulled me into his arms and covered my mouth with his. He forced his tongue between my teeth and kissed me so hard and so deep that it took my breath away.

Then he scooped me up, carried me to the bed and fucked me again, driving all other thoughts from my mind.

After he finished, I fell asleep with Jack's powerful arms wrapped around me.

When the sun rose, I slipped out of Jack's bed and walked through the entire villa. I couldn't find him to say good-bye. I didn't have time hang around, so I found my clothes on the porch where I'd left them, pulled them on and headed down to the beach. Nine steps into my descent I stepped on broken glass, and, at first, I thought it was my broken shot glass from the night before. Then I looked down and saw an empty picture frame—the same frame that had once held the photograph of Jack's handsome lover.

I hesitated. Jack was gone. The picture was gone. I was out of time. There was nothing I could do but go back to Jamie.

I walked south along the beach, back to the cottage.

As soon as I pushed open the door, Jamie shouted, "Where the *hell* have you been?"

"I went for a walk."

"All night?"

I didn't respond.

"You went to see him, didn't you?"

I didn't deny it. Instead, I finished packing. Then I had the front desk call us a cab. When it came, we shoved our bags into the trunk and sat in the backseat as far from one another as we could get. I sat seaside and stared out the window.

Halfway to the airport, a long stretch of the road

hugged the shoreline, with only a thin stretch of white sand between the road and the water. Ahead of us, at the point where the road turned inland again, an ambulance and a trio of police cars with their lights flashing blocked the road. A dozen people had gathered on the beach, watching two paramedics working over someone or something.

A lone police officer stood in the road directing traffic. As the cab slowed, our driver rolled his window down and asked what all the commotion was about.

"A body washed ashore," the officer said. "Looks like a tourist got caught in the tides."

A tourist? Thin blond? Muscular brunet? I craned my neck to see but the cab moved forward and the crowd below shifted position to close the gap between people. I never learned the answer.

The flight home next to Jamie was long and uncomfortable, and we barely spoke a dozen words between us. As soon as the cab deposited us in front of our dormitory, we went our separate ways. A few days later Jamie dropped out of school.

I never saw him again. But I often revisit the image of a perfect man emerging from the sea.

SMOOTH STROKES

David turned from the mirror, satisfied that he had finally wrestled his hair into place.

"You always take so long to primp?"

David hadn't realized anyone else was in the locker room and he nearly jumped out of his skin. He continued turning until he found the source of the question, a dark-haired gentleman at least ten years his senior leaning against the far wall near the exit.

"It's the chlorine," David said. "It makes my hair frizz."

"I saw." The man pushed himself off the wall and stepped toward David. "I watched you swim. You have a smooth stroke."

"You like to watch?"

"Not when I have other options." The man introduced himself as Clive and held out his hand.

David grasped the older man's hand and felt a grip as firm as his own.

"You finished here?" Clive asked. "I know a place we could get a drink."

David hesitated. He'd never been one to hook up with men he met in locker rooms.

"It's OK," Clive said. "I won't bite."

"One drink," David said, "and I might."

Clive smiled.

Thirty minutes later they were seated under an umbrella at an outdoor cafe, sipping wine and enjoying the cool evening breeze blowing uptown from the lake. Music from a jazz band playing two doors down drifted past and David finally relaxed enough that he could appreciate his new companion's ruggedly handsome good looks.

Up close David could see the tiny threads of silver highlighting Clive's raven black hair and he could see the sparkle of intelligence in Clive's hazel eyes. He felt a stirring in his groin that he had not felt in many months, and he welcomed the physical evidence that he was still a sexual being. Derek had been the last man to affect him this way, and Derek had walked out on New Year's Day.

"Why haven't I met you before now?" Clive asked.

"I'm only here for the summer," David explained.

"Why only the summer?" Clive sipped from his glass.

"I'm interning at Bowker & Smith."

The older man nearly spit out his wine. "You're working at B&S? I thought they stopped using interns after the Getty incident."

David looked a question across the table.

"Nobody's told you about Getty?" Clive asked. He leaned back and examined the young man before continuing. "Getty was about your age, but not nearly so handsome. He'd been interning at Bowker & Smith a couple of weeks when Bowker senior took a liking to him. Bowker took Getty to dinner, to the symphony, to a few gallery openings, out on his boat, and to his penthouse. There was talk that Bowker was grooming Getty for something big, and maybe he was, if you believe the other rumors about Bowker."

"Other rumors?" David asked.

"Let's just say that his wallet isn't the only big thing in Bowker's pants." Clive caught the waiter's attention and ordered a second glass of wine for each of them. He waited until the wine arrived before continuing his story. "At least four people saw Getty get on the elevator with Bowker the night he disappeared. Nobody's seen him since."

"I work for Bowker," David said.

"Of course, you already said that."

"No, I don't just work for the company, I report directly to Bowker."

Clive leaned forward. "Now that's interesting."

"And he's taken me to dinner twice and once to a play."

"Anything unusual happen?"

David had been hit on by many men over the years, so he didn't think it unusual that Bowker had put a hand on his knee or even that Bowker's hand had slid up the inside of his thigh during their second dinner. What was unusual was that Bowker had not actually propositioned him. He explained all this to Clive.

"Do you think he plans to ask you to his penthouse?"

"I—I don't know," David said. "I don't know what he has in mind."

"But what if he does?" Clive leaned forward and placed one hand on David's forearm, causing David's cock to swell and his temperature to rise. "Will you go?"

David saw the intensity in Clive's gaze.

"Some things you just have to do to get ahead," David said, not quite answering the question, "I'm not in a relationship right now, and knowing a man like Mr. Bowker could only do good things for my career. What's it to you? We've only just met."

Clive reached into his back pocket and retrieved a well-worn leather wallet. He flipped it open to reveal a badge on one side and a photo I.D. on the other. "We need somebody on the inside. We think that somebody might be you."

David's cock withered. Just when he'd begun to consider the real possibility of a sexual encounter with the handsome man sitting across from him, that possibility had been dashed. "Me? Why me?"

"You're Bowker's type—young, handsome, and willing to do whatever—or whoever—it takes to get ahead," Clive explained as he pulled his wallet back and returned it to his pocket. "And you're already on the inside."

"What's in it for me?"

Clive mentioned the $25,000 reward Getty's parents had offered for information leading to the return of their son, the state's willingness to guarantee him admission to and provide him a free ride through graduate school if he remained a student in the state's university system, and a guaranteed job with the state upon graduation.

David spun his wine glass slowly, thinking carefully about how this might impact his career. He'd already planned to fuck Bowker if the opportunity arose, but Clive's proposal upped the stakes considerably. "You'll put all this in writing?"

"Of course."

David finally nodded. "Then I'm in."

The police fitted him with a wire and for the next few days recorded every mundane conversation he had with his coworkers at Bowker & Smith. Each evening Clive visited his apartment to discuss the day's events and suggest ways David could entice Bowker into accelerating his seduction of David.

Friday afternoon, after David had been called into Bowker's office to discuss an insignificant project that David was working on, Bowker placed his hand on David's ass and gave it a playful squeeze.

David knew the time was appropriate to push just a little bit. "You keep teasing me, Mr. Bowker," he said, "but if you wait much longer summer will be over and I'll be gone."

"How about tomorrow, then," Bowker said. "I'll have my car pick you up at eight, we'll have dinner, and then we can go to my penthouse to...discuss your future...see what openings may be available...and see if you're a good fit."

David smiled. "I think I'd like that."

He didn't have to report the conversation to Clive because the police investigator had heard the recording before they spoke that evening in David's apartment. By then, the microphone had been turned off and their conversation was private.

"Are you going to be okay with this?" Clive asked.

David eyed the dark-haired man standing next to him in the kitchenette of his tiny apartment. He had been thinking about Clive all week, waking up in the middle of the night with rock hard erections that he had to wrestle into submission with the help of some hand lotion before returning to sleep. He was unsure if the attraction was more than physical, but the idea that the police investigator might control his fate was certainly a turn-on. Clive was just as powerful as Bowker, but in a different way, and David had always been attracted to powerful men. He said, "I'll be fine."

Clive reached out and brushed a lock of hair away from David's eyes. "I worry about you."

David waved his index finger toward the tiny microphone resting on the kitchen table. "You sure that thing's turned off?"

After Clive nodded, David captured Clive's wrist and drew Clive's hand to his face. He wrapped his lips around Clive's two middle fingers and sucked them into his mouth, watching the police investigator's eyes widen in surprise. He sucked hard and watched as Clive shifted uncomfortably, the crotch of his pants expanding to accommodate the growing erection inside.

When David finally released his oral grip on Clive's

fingers, the police investigator cleared his throat and protested, "We have to keep our relationship professional."

"It's too late for that," David told him as he unbuttoned his shirt and revealed his broad, hairless chest and washboard abs. He was built like a swimmer and he kept his body, except for what he covered with a swimming cap, hairless to reduce drag in the water. "You want me. I know you want me. I knew it from the moment you spoke to me in the locker room, but you haven't admitted it to yourself because of what you need me to do for you."

Clive reached out and placed the flat of his hand on David's chest, holding the younger man at arm's length.

"This may be your last chance," David continued.

Clive didn't reply. Instead, he dropped his hand from David's chest to his belt and pulled him close. He covered David's mouth with his and kissed the younger man hard and deep.

As they kissed, they fumbled with one another's belts, buttons, and zippers, and soon Clive's slacks and boxer briefs were around his ankles and David was on his knees in front of the police investigator.

The cop's cock was long, thick, and hard. David wrapped one hand around the turgid shaft and his lips around the spongy soft cock head. As he slowly pistoned his hand along the length of Clive's shaft, he painted Clive's cock head with his tongue, licking away drops of pre-come. David slowly lowered his face toward Clive's crotch, taking in the cop's entire length before drawing back until just Clive's cock head remained in his mouth.

He did it again and again. Clive's hips began to move back and forth as David face-fucked him, and soon Clive couldn't hold back any longer. He grabbed the countertop behind him as he thrust forward one last time and fired hot spunk against the back of David's throat.

David swallowed every drop and then licked Clive's cock clean. After David stood, Clive stepped out of the clothing tangled at his feet, and David led him into the bedroom. They finished undressing.

David had a new tube of lube on his nightstand and Clive reached for it. He squeezed a dollop onto his fingers and then massaged David's backside, teasing David's ass hole as he slathered it with lube. As David bent over the bed, Clive pressed one finger into David.

David spread his legs and Clive was able to slip a second finger into him.

"Stop teasing me," David whispered huskily. "Take me now."

Clive's cock had regained its former stature, so he stepped forward and pressed his cock head against David's lube-slicked sphincter. He grabbed David's hips and pressed forward, easing his cock into the young man. Then he drew back and pressed forward, driving faster and harder.

David's cock was hard, and he wrapped his hand around his stiff shaft, fist-fucking himself as Clive took him from behind. Soon they matched rhythms.

David came first, spewing spunk across the cover.

Then Clive came. With one last, powerful thrust, he

sank his cock all the way into David and filled him with come.

A few minutes later they collapsed on the bed. They spooned, with Clive behind David, and they talked about everything except what would happen the following day.

David fell asleep but Clive remained holding him until a few minutes after midnight when he slipped from David's bed and pulled on his clothes. David heard him, rolled over, and opened one eye. He said, "You don't have to leave."

"Yes, I do. You'll need your rest if you're going to pull this thing off tonight." Clive said. He bent over the bed and kissed David's forehead. "We'll have plenty of time together when this is over."

David was still thinking about Clive when Bowker's driver arrived that evening to take him to dinner, and he wondered if he wasn't somehow about to cheat on his new lover. Then he pushed that thought out of his mind. What he was about to do was business, and nothing but business, and he would do whatever he had to do to get ahead.

Bowker was well into his sixties, with a mane of gray hair that he swept backward from his forehead to his shoulders, and he wore custom-tailored suits that cost more than a semester's tuition at David's college. He was waiting at a private table in a back room at Antonio's, and he rose when David entered the room.

"Come," he said. "Sit."

David joined Bowker at the table, followed his boss's

lead when ordering filet mignon, baked potato, and house salad, and he nursed his wine. He needed a little to relax but did not want so much as to become inebriated.

Bowker was effusive in his compliments, buttering up David and telling him about all the career opportunities that were sure to come his way in the near future. "I've had my eye on you since the day you joined the firm," Bowker said. "You're bright, handsome, a real go-getter. We need—I need—a man like you."

"Thank you," David told him. "I appreciate any opportunities that...come...my way."

The older man roared with laughter. "Then you'll certainly appreciate the big opportunity I'll be presenting tonight."

David smiled. Things were going as expected.

They both declined dessert. Then the chauffer took them less than half a mile to Bowker's building, where they rode the elevator to the penthouse.

Bowker led David to the bedroom. "Make yourself comfortable. I'll just be a minute."

Bowker stepped into the adjoining bathroom without closing the door and David watched the older man's reflection in the mirror. His boss opened a pill bottle, shook a little blue pill into the palm of his hand, and then swallowed it dry.

By the time Bowker returned to the bedroom, David had removed his shoes and was unbuttoning his shirt. Bowker crossed the bedroom and flipped down the bed covers to reveal blue silk sheets. Then he stripped, folded his clothes and hung them on the clothing butler.

Bowker had the biggest cock David had ever seen up close and personal, rivaling even some that he'd seen in magazines and on videos. By then the Viagra had begun to affect the older man and Bowker's cock began to rise.

David finished undressing, careful to place his shirt on top of the rest of his clothes, folded so that the microphone hidden in his collar button wasn't obscured by anything.

David felt Bowker's gaze crawl over his body, and he took advantage of the moment to pose seductively.

Bowker rounded the bed and grabbed David's arm. He pulled the younger man into his arms and shoved his tongue into David's moth, surprising David. David felt Bowker's erection pressing against his abdomen and he shoved one hand between them. He wrapped his fist around Bowker's cock.

Bowker pushed David to his knees and David took the hint. He wrapped his lips around Bower's cock, surprised at just how big the older man's mushroom cap was. While David painted it with his tongue, Bowker pressed his hands against the back of David's head.

David couldn't take more than half of Bowker's cock into his mouth without gagging, but he bobbed up and down his boss's stiff shaft as best he could.

After a few minutes, Bowker pulled David to his feet, spun him around, and pushed him forward so that David bent over the bed. Bowker grabbed David's hips and shoved his cock between David's ass cheeks. Then he pressed his saliva-slickened cock head against David's sphincter and thrust his hips forward.

Without lube, without even a moment to relax and prepare for what was happening, David was surprised. His eyes opened wide, and he sucked in his breath as Bowker's cock drove into him.

He wasn't particularly aroused by Bowker's treatment and his own cock barely rose beyond half-mast. Bowker reached around him and grabbed his cock. When the older man realized that David wasn't fully erect, he snorted derisively and released his grip on David's cock.

"What's wrong?" he asked. "Can't you handle a real man?"

David bit this bottom lip but didn't respond. He accepted every one of Bowker's powerful thrusts, pushing back against his boss with feigned enthusiasm.

Bowker threw his head back and came with a roar. He fired hot spunk deep into David's ass and he held the young man in place until his cock stopped throbbing. Then he pulled his softening cock free with an audible pop and pushed David forward onto the bed.

David rolled over and lay back on the king-size bed. He folded his hands behind his head and asked, "Now what?"

Bowker sat on the edge of the bed and pulled on his blue silk boxers. He turned. "Excuse me?"

"You had your way with me," David continued. "Now what do I get out of this?"

Bowker laughed. "You don't get shit. Monday morning I put you in the mail room and you're grateful I let you finish your internship."

"Is that the deal you offered Getty?"

"Getty?" Bowker stood and crossed the room to he clothing butler. "That little punk thought he could blackmail me. He didn't know who he was dealing with."

"So, what'd you do to him?"

"He went swimming in a pair of cement shoes." Bowker pulled on his slacks.

"He's in the lake?"

Bowker glared at David. "You keep asking questions and maybe you'll find out exactly where he's at."

"So those are my choices?" David asked. He was a good swimmer, but he knew he wouldn't get far wearing cement flippers. "The mail room or the lake?"

"I couldn't have put it better myself." Then Bowker's eyes narrowed. "You wearing a wire?"

"Do I look like I'm wearing anything at all?"

Bowker stared at the young man for a full minute, neither of them speaking.

"Get dressed and get out of here," Bowker said. He pulled out his wallet and tossed a hundred-dollar bill on the bed. "Take a cab home."

David dressed and let himself out of the penthouse. He rode the elevator downstairs and crossed the lobby to the building's exit. He walked to the curb to hail a cab and one immediately pulled to the curb in front of him.

He slid into the backseat and gave the driver his address. They were half a block away before David realized Clive was driving the cab.

"Did you get what you needed?" he asked.

"Perfect," Clive assured him. "You did perfect."

Their reflected gazes met in the rearview mirror.

Clive asked, "Are you okay?"

"I will be," David assured him. He leaned forward and put his hand on the cop's shoulder. "But it might take a while."

Without removing his attention from the road, Clive reached one hand over his shoulder and patted David's hand. "I'll be here for you, however long it takes."

David returned to school that fall, $25,000 richer with the money from Getty's parents in his bank account. Bowker's trial was still months away, but the outcome seemed a foregone conclusion after the police recovered Getty's body from the lake and found DNA evidence tying Getty to Bowker's boat.

One afternoon, David walked into the locker room from the university's indoor pool and found a dark-haired gentleman at least ten years his senior waiting for him. He didn't usually hook up with men in locker rooms, but he made an exception this time.

"Do you still have a smooth stroke?" Clive asked.

"Who would know better than you?" David asked as the cop pulled him into his arms and they kissed.

MEAT AND POTATOES

I shot the lying motherfucker fifteen times. I had to reload twice to do it, and I would have continued shooting Thompson if I hadn't ran out of bullets.

When my ears stopped ringing, I heard a polite cough. That's when I realized someone was standing behind me. My rock-hard cock instantly shriveled.

I turned and found myself facing a bald-headed behemoth whose thick, muscular arms were covered in black and blue tattoos of no discernable pattern. He wore scuffed black motorcycle boots, faded blue jeans, and a sleeveless black T-shirt tight as a second skin. He held a sawed-off double-barrel shotgun in one hand and half a beignet in the other. "You done yet?"

I swallowed hard and nodded.

"Then get out of the way."

I stepped aside and the man mountain emptied both barrels of the shotgun into Thompson's remains.

"I always wanted to do that," the behemoth said. He stuffed the last of the beignet into his mouth, broke the shotgun open, and reloaded. "Let's go."

"Where?"

"Any place but here, citizen," he said. "The cops'll be coming soon." I followed him out of Thompson's two-bedroom bungalow and, as we crossed the porch, he asked, "How'd you get here?"

"Thompson drove."

"Then I guess you'll need to ride with me." He led me down the steps and across the weed-choked lawn to a candy apple red Harley-Davidson Shovelhead with apehanger handlebars and chopper forks leaning on its kickstand. After stuffing the sawed-off into a custom-made leather holster, he straddled the bike. "Mind riding bitch?"

I shook my head.

A moment later he kick-started the engine and the familiar *potato-potato-potato* Harley-Davidson sound filled my ears. I shoved Thompson's revolver into my jacket pocket, climbed on behind the behemoth, and tried to wrap my arms around him. I couldn't. Then we were off, down the street and around the corner from the dead man's house.

I wore penny loafers, chinos, and a polo shirt under my windbreaker. I hadn't bothered to retrieve my socks and I had no idea where my briefs had gone. I did have a wad of cash in my pants pocket, money I'd taken from Thompson's dresser before I'd shot him. The rumble of the motorcycle between my thighs gave me a rock-hard erection that rubbed against the inside of my chinos and pressed against the behemoth's lower back. If he noticed the pressure from my cock and from the wad of bills, he didn't say anything.

But I probably couldn't have heard him if he had.

We rode across town, weaving in and out of traffic until we came to another neighborhood that might as well have been around the corner from the dead man's house for all the difference twenty miles made. We wheeled up onto the sidewalk in front of a ramshackle bungalow that might have once been painted white. The house had a wheelchair ramp extending from the porch to the sidewalk and he drove the Shovelhead straight up the ramp, stopping on the porch only long enough to unlock the front door and for me to get off before wheeling the bike into the living room and locking the door behind us.

My host wasn't big on decoration. The only things in the living room other than the Shovelhead were a red thirteen-drawer Craftsman tool cart on wheels, a flat screen TV, and a black leather couch held together with gray duct tape and covered on one end by a black leather jacket with his motorcycle club's insignia on the back.

The man mountain put one hand on my shoulder and propelled me down the hallway. "Take a shower, citizen. Try to wash the stink off."

I did as I was told, and when I stepped out of the shower twenty minutes later, I discovered that my clothes were gone—my clothes and everything in my pockets. I wrapped a threadbare blue towel around my slim hips and walked through the house until I found my host sitting at the yellow Formica and chrome kitchen table, Thompson's revolver in pieces in front of him, the wad of Thompson's cash near his left elbow, and my wallet, keys, and pocket change piled on my side of the table. My wallet was open, and my driver's license stuck half out of it.

The behemoth had taken off his T-shirt and I saw the word "Meat" tattooed across his chest in six-inch-tall black Olde English script. I pointed at his chest. "That your name?"

"Good as any other," he replied. He held up the disassembled revolver. "Where'd you get this?"

"In Thompson's nightstand, same as the bullets," I told him. "Where are my clothes?"

"Washing machine." He motioned toward the refrigerator. "Get me a beer. Get yourself one, too."

Inside the Frigidaire I found a half-empty twenty-four pack of Dixie and pulled two cans from it. I returned to the table with a beer in each hand. When I put Meat's on the table in front of him, I realized he hadn't just removed his T-shirt; he was butt-ass naked under the table.

"Where are *your* clothes?"

"With yours." As if to punctuate his statement, the sink drain gurgled and water from the washing machine began backing up into it.

Meat opened his beer, swallowed half the can, and then he finished cleaning the revolver and reassembled it. He watched me the entire time, taking his measure of me the way I was taking my measure of him.

"Got a little something for you," Meat said. He pushed back his chair and stood. My eyes widened in surprise. Many of the bulked-up men I'd been with were steroid abusers, with shriveled balls, limp dicks, and acne on their ass. Not Meat. He'd built his muscles the old-fashioned way and his semi-erect cock was a one-eyed python rising from a tangled nest of black hair.

I licked my lips, wetting them with just the tip of my tongue. Worse than being a lying motherfucker, Thompson had been a terrible lay, barely able to sustain the pitiable little erection he'd managed even after I'd spent half an hour sucking like a Hoover, and I was still horny as a virgin on Viagra.

The threadbare towel fell away from my hips as I dropped to my knees on the linoleum floor and kissed the swollen head of my host's cock, teasing his come slit with my tongue. I licked all the way around the ridge of his glans and then used the tip of my tongue to trace a wet line down the underside of his engorged cock to his heavy ball sac. I sucked his nuts into my mouth and sucked them hard, stretching his sac and collecting curly black hair between my teeth. Then my tongue raced back up the length of his cock and I took his cock head into my mouth. I swallowed more and more of it until I thought I couldn't take any more. Meat thought different. He grabbed the back of my head, his thick fingers threading through my blond hair, and face-fucked me.

When he finally came, he came hard, and come exploded against the back of my throat. I couldn't swallow fast enough and some of his come leaked from the corners my mouth and down my chin. As he stepped back, pulling his cock from my oral cavity, I wiped my chin with the back of my hand.

He pulled me to my feet and propelled me down the

hall to the bedroom, which was as sparsely furnished as his living room, with an unmade king-size bed filling most of the available space. The nightstand held a lamp without a shade, a clock radio, and a tube of lube. Three plastic clothesbaskets filled with folded clothing—underwear, T-shirts, and socks—lined one wall. Dirty clothes were piled in one corner. The closet door stood half-open, and I could see the sawed-off in its holster along with several handguns hanging from a pegboard mounted to the back wall. Before I could crane my neck for a better look at Meat's armory, he bent me over the side of the bed and reached for his lube. He slathered the slick goo over his middle finger and then began stroking my sphincter. I spread my legs, opening my ass to his digital manipulation. He pressed the tip of his finger against my anal opening and pushed. By the time he had his finger buried to the first knuckle, my cock started to rise. By the time he had his entire finger up my ass, my cock was hard as a rock.

Meat reached around, wrapped one fist around my cock, and began to pump so vigorously I thought he was going to snap my cock off. At the same time, he was jerking me off, he was finger-fucking my ass, and after the fiasco with Thompson the previous evening I was glad to be with a real man.

Before I could stop myself—not that I wanted to—I came, spewing come all over Meat's bed sheet. My legs turned to gelatin, and I thought my knees would buckle. Meat pulled his finger from my ass and grabbed my hips to keep me upright. The python between his legs had awoken again and he pressed his cock head against my butt pucker. He had prepped me, had lubed my hole quite thoroughly, had stretched my opening with this thick finger, but I wasn't truly prepared for what came next.

He drove his long, thick cock into my ass and didn't stop until every last bit of it was inside me. He drew back until only his cock head remained inside, and then he drove forward again. He held my hips so tight he left ten fingertip-sized bruises that I didn't notice until later. I also didn't notice the pain of his tight grip because my attention was fully concentrated on the pain and pleasure of the ass fucking I was getting. He thrust savagely for a full five minutes, time I watched count down on the clock radio, and then he fired a load nearly as voluminous as the one he'd popped in my mouth.

He held me until his cock stopped spasming, and then he pulled away and let me drop face-first on the dirty sheet. He left me there and disappeared into the bathroom. When he returned, he threw a damp washcloth—the one I'd used earlier to clean off gunpowder and Thompson's blood—and told me to clean up.

After Meat moved our clothes from the washing machine to the dryer, we returned to the kitchen still naked, opened two more Dixies and a sack of day-old beignets, and sat at the yellow Formica and chrome table where we'd sat before we'd fucked.

After downing half his beer, Meat asked, "Why'd you shoot Thompson?"

"He promised me two hundred for the night. Then he refused to pay."

"So, you took his money and shot him?" He retrieved a beignet from the bag.

"Yeah."

"How many times?"

"Fifteen.

"Once would have been enough."

I shrugged. "Why'd *you* shoot him?"

"Seemed like a good idea at the time." He shoved the beignet into his mouth, chewed, and swallowed.

"Why were you even there?"

"I'm the MC's sergeant at arms," Meat explained. "The club's enforcer. If somebody doesn't do something they're supposed to do, I remind them of their responsibilities. Thompson was behind in his dues." He licked confectioner's sugar off one thick finger—the same finger he'd had up my ass—and used it to nudge the wad of bills I'd taken from Thompson's dresser. "Looks like he was holding out on us."

"You ever kill anybody?"

The behemoth sat up straight as if to remind me of his imposing physique. "Never needed to."

I looked a question at him.

"Thompson was the first guy I ever shot," he said, "but I'm pretty sure he was already dead when I arrived."

Thompson wasn't the first guy I'd ever shot, but I didn't tell Meat that.

He peeled a pair of Benjamins off the roll and tossed them at me. "Here's what Thompson owes you," he said. "The rest goes to the club."

I put the Benjamins in my wallet and pushed my

driver's license back into place. Then I stood. "Think my clothes are dry?"

"You planning to leave?"

"Might as well." I held up my wallet. "I got what I wanted."

"Don't do anything stupid after you leave here, Kyle," Meat threatened. "I know where you live."

He had seen my driver's license, but it didn't matter. It was a forgery. "I haven't lived there in years."

"Yeah?" he said. "Where do you live?"

"Around," I said. "Here and there. Depends."

"Depends on how many tricks you turn?"

I shrugged. I let him think he'd nailed it.

"I could use somebody around here," he said. "You looking for something steady?"

"Sure," I told him. "Why not?"

I could ride bitch for a day or a week or a month or a year. Sooner or later, I'd figure out where the big motherfucker kept his money and where he kept his ammo and how soundly he slept. And with all those guns in his closet I could do more than shoot him fifteen times. I'd let him fuck me until I was ready to fuck him over.

I smiled at the thought. Bikers were so easy.

Meat thought I was smiling at him, and he took me back to the bedroom.

RUN FOR THE BORDER

My sphincter tightened and my balls retreated into my body cavity when the passenger door of my Dodge Dakota opened, a canvas duffel bag hit the floorboard next to the sack of things I'd purchased only minutes earlier, and a hardbodied bald man wearing dusty black work boots, dirty faded jeans, a blood-stained white wife-beater, and tattoo sleeves slid in next to me, pressed the barrel of a snub-nose revolver against my temple and commanded, "Drive."

"But the light's—"

He cocked the hammer and I accelerated through the red light, causing the driver of a minivan approaching the intersection from the south to slam on the brakes. The minivan narrowly missed the ass end of my truck and bucked up onto the sidewalk on the far side of the intersection.

"Where?" I asked.

My passenger uncocked the revolver, lowered it to his lap, and rested it on a bulge at his crotch that was either a roll of quarters or some serious man meat. "Just go straight until I say otherwise."

I ventured a glance into the rearview mirror and caught a reflection of blue eyes so pale they almost had no color at all. I returned my attention to the road ahead of me, a road that led directly to the Interstate, and I didn't say another word until my passenger asked, "You got a name?"

"Daryl," I lied. "Daryl Johnson. You?"

"Not important," he said. "You got a cell phone, Daryl?"

I admitted that I did.

"Give it to me."

I took my iPhone from my shirt pocket and handed it to him. He looked at it for a moment and then threw it out the open passenger window.

"Jesus!" I turned to face him. He wasn't actually bald, though he had shaved his head a few days earlier and had only sparse salt-and-pepper regrowth covering his sunburned pate. "You know how much that cost?"

My passenger lifted his revolver. "More important," he said. "What's it worth?"

Not my life, I decided. Though I had lived in the city for more than a dozen years, I had grown up in a God-fearing, gun-toting, small-town redneck family and I understood the persuasive power of the snub-nosed revolver in my passenger's fist. I concentrated on driving until he asked another question.

"You married? Got a family? Anybody waiting for you at home?"

I shook my head. My boyfriend had moved out of my downtown loft two weeks earlier after spending more than an hour listing every one of my perceived flaws, from lack of spontaneity to passive-aggressiveness.

"So, what do you do that you need a truck?"

"Nothing."

"Nothing?"

"You're not from around here, are you?" I asked. In Texas, pickup trucks are as common as concealed carry permits—I knew because I had both—and the Dakota was my third consecutive truck since I began driving. I hand-washed and detailed it every Saturday, something even my holier-than-thou ex hadn't done with his Prius. "Everybody in Texas drives trucks. It's a state law."

"You trying to be funny?"

I shrugged as we rounded a curve and the highway came into view.

"Get on the Interstate."

"Which way?"

"South," he said. "Toward Mexico."

I glanced at the fuel gauge. "I don't have enough gas to reach the border."

He kicked the canvas bag. "We'll be fine."

"What's in the bag?"

"Gas money."

"Where'd you get it?"

"Drug dealer," he said. "But he won't miss it. He's beyond missing anything."

"You kill him?"

My passenger didn't respond so I ventured a glance at him. I asked, "What happened to your car?"

"You ask a lot of questions, Daryl," he said. "It might be better if you didn't."

I kept quiet. Once we were clear of the city and the southern suburbs my passenger made me exit the Interstate and take a smaller highway headed south. He adjusted position several times, apparently trying to get comfortable, and finally kicked the sack containing my purchases from earlier in the evening.

He reached down for the sack and opened it. From it he pulled two gay porn magazines, a vibrating dildo, and a tube of lube. After examining everything carefully, he stared hard at me for a moment. Then he shoved it all back in the sack and dropped the sack on the floor next to his duffel bag, where it had been ever since he'd climbed into my truck back in the city. We didn't talk about what he'd found, but I knew from his reaction to it that he was reappraising me.

The more time passed the more comfortable I felt. I knew that, one way or the other, I was sitting on my salvation and all I needed was the right opportunity. I just didn't know when it would come.

When night collapsed upon us a bit later, I flicked on the headlights. Another hour passed with only the sound of the engine and the tires humming against the pavement to keep us company. We hadn't passed through any towns for at least half an hour when the pressure in my bladder got the best of me.

I said, "I need to piss."

At his direction, I took the next exit onto a Farm-to-Market road in the middle of nowhere, drove a mile or so until the highway was no longer in sight and found a dirt road that led into the scrub. Several hundred yards from the Farm-to-Market road, I stopped the truck. My passenger made me shut off the engine and hand him the keys.

"You need to piss," he said as he motioned with the revolver. "Go piss."

With only the moonlight to guide me, I climbed out of the truck, walked around to the passenger side, and faced away from the road, out of sight of any vehicles that might venture past. I heard the truck's passenger door open as I pulled my cock from my jeans and let loose a long stream.

A second stream joined mine and, after I finished and tucked my cock away, I ventured a glance at my traveling companion's equipment. The bulge I'd seen in his jeans when he'd first climbed into my truck wasn't a roll of quarters after all. My glance turned into an appreciate stare.

He noticed. "What are you staring at?"

"Your cock."

He still held the snub-nosed revolver in his right hand, so he used his left hand to shake away the last drops of urine. "You like a big pecker?"

My ex had only been gone two weeks, but it had been months since we'd been intimate in any way, and I had planned to attend to my own needs later that evening. That's why I'd purchased the dildo, the lube, and the magazines. The man wagging his cock in front of me was so unlike my ex in every way—so brute-like and so unlike the men I usually found attractive—that I was surprised I was getting aroused. Maybe it was my sexual drought or maybe it was the thrill of being carjacked at gunpoint and forced to chauffeur my abductor toward Mexico. Either way, I wanted him. I said, "Yes. I do."

He glanced around, saw nothing of interest, and said, "Get on your knees."

After I did as instructed, my abductor stepped close. He slapped my face with his flaccid cock, whipping it against one cheek and then against the other. When he attempted to slap me with it a third time, I turned my head and caught it between my lips. I quickly sucked in the spongy soft helmet head and hooked my teeth behind the glans so that he couldn't easily pull away.

Surprised, he quickly brought the revolver up and pointed it in my face. Staring into the barrel of the revolver I was also staring into the chambers of the cylinder. The revolver was so close that I noticed in the dim light something I hadn't noticed earlier, and I realized my abductor had lost his position of power.

He grabbed the back of my head with his free hand and shoved his still-flaccid cock completely into my mouth before he drew back. I hoovered his cock to erection, sucking hard as he shoved his hips forward and pulled them back, and when his thick cock was fully erect it was too long for me to take its entirety. That didn't stop him from trying to shove the head of his cock down my throat.

As he face-fucked me, the teeth of his zipper

scratched my nose, my cheeks, and my lips, and the pain only increased my desire for him.

He began pumping his hips faster, and he grabbed the back of my head with his gun hand, the butt of the handgun smashed against the back of my head.

As he face-fucked me, my cock tented the front of my jeans. I wanted to release it and take it in my hand, but there wasn't time. My abductor came, filling my mouth with hot spunk. I swallowed as fast I could but wasn't fast enough. Some of his spunk dribbled from the corner of my lips and dripped to the ground near my knees.

He pulled his cock from my mouth and waved the revolver at me. "Go," he said. "Get that lube from the truck."

I pushed myself to my feet and stepped over to the truck. I found the sack halfway under the passenger seat and I pulled the tube of lube from the bag.

Once I had it, my passenger waved me to the back of the truck. He had me lower the tailgate and then lower my pants. He made me squeeze lube onto my hand and reach behind my ball sac to lube my own ass.

Then he made me lube his come-covered cock, which rapidly regained its former stature, before he had me turn around and bend over the open tailgate. He stepped up behind me and for a moment I worried that he might stick the barrel of his gun into my ass.

He didn't. He also didn't bother to drop his pants when he pressed the head of his cock against my tight sphincter. I easily opened to him as he sank his thick shaft deep inside me, but his zipper scratched the cheeks of my ass just as it had scratched my face a few minutes earlier.

As he drew back and pressed forward, I braced myself with one hand and grabbed my cock with the other. Soon my pistoning hand matched the rhythm of his cock driving in and out of my ass, my pace quickening when his pace did.

I came first, sending a thick stream of spunk against the back of my pickup truck.

My abductor slammed into me three more times and then he came, filling my ass with hot spunk. We remained stuck together, catching our breath, until we heard something rustling through the scrub.

He pulled away and spun around. "What was that?"

I had been raised far from the city and hadn't been startled, but I knew from my abductor's reaction that he was a city boy clear through to his bones.

"Nothing to worry about." I pulled up my pants. "If we don't bother whatever it is, it won't bother us."

He used his free hand to tuck his cock into his pants and pull his zipper up.

I closed the tailgate and we each walked around the truck to our respective sides.

We climbed into the truck and, with the revolver still pointed at me, he handed me the keys. They slipped from my fingers and dropped to the floorboard. The entire time I had been driving toward Mexico I had been sitting on my salvation. As I reached down for the key ring, I reached under my seat and pulled my fully permitted automatic pistol from the holster affixed there.

I sat upright, drove the barrel of the automatic into my passenger's gut, and said, "Get out."

His eyes widened in surprise, but he kept his cool. The handgun he had pointed at me never wavered. He said, "Looks like we have a stalemate."

"You go first," I said. "Pull the trigger."

He did and the revolver's hammer snapped down multiple times, slamming the firing pin against spent bullet cases, as I had known it would when I looked into the bullet-less chambers while giving him a blowjob. Whatever he had done before he climbed into my truck had used every bullet, leaving only spent cases behind.

He swore.

"Get out," I repeated. "Leave the bag."

He eyed me, perhaps calculating his odds. Then he slid from the truck and stood where I could see him.

"Take your boots off and throw them in the back."

As he did as instructed I used my left hand to key the ignition. Then I shift the truck into gear, spun the wheel, and pressed the accelerator. The Dakota spun in a half circle, causing the passenger door to slam shut and gravel to pepper my abductor.

I drove away, his come leaking from my zipper-scratched ass to stain my underwear, but I didn't care. If my abductor survived the night in the scrub, if he managed to walk barefoot back to the highway and catch a ride, and if he remembered the name I had given him, it would lead him to my ex. They deserved each other.

Like my ex said. I'm passive aggressive.

QUEER BAIT

I pressed the business end of my .38 into the sweet spot behind Joe Mulligan's left earlobe and cocked the trigger. "Raise your fist again and I'll squeeze."

Mulligan's an ex-cop built like a boxer, with bulging biceps and ham-sized fists, and he'd been pounding on a thin young man in the alley behind Chartreuse. Mulligan loosened his fingers and lowered his hands to his sides.

"Get in the car," I told the bloody young blond collapsed against the brick wall. "Now!"

He stumbled to my Taurus and slid into the passenger seat. After shoving my revolver into my shoulder rig, I joined him in the car, keyed the ignition, and drove away. I only glanced in the rearview mirror once, but Mulligan had disappeared by then.

Six blocks closer to my office, the blond said, "Thanks."

Without looking at him, I asked, "You got a name?"

"William," he said. "Bill. Billy. Whatever you want to call me is fine."

"What'd you do to piss off Mulligan?"

"Told him he had a nice ass."

I glanced across the darkness of the car. "That would do it."

Billy folded his arms across his thin chest and slumped against the passenger door. "Figures I'd try to pick up a Neanderthal with self-image issues."

My dick stirred in my pants. I did my best to ignore it. "You always hit on older men?"

"Not always," Billy said.

"You need to be careful," I told him. "Guys like Mulligan go looking for sweet little things like you. That's how they get their rocks off."

"What about you?" Billy asked. "How do you get your rocks off?"

I ignored Billy's question, signaled for a left turn, and soon had my Taurus parked in the garage next to the building housing my office. "If you want to clean up, you can use the washroom in my office."

I'd parked near a security floodlight and the inside of the Taurus was lit up like an airport runway. Billy examined me for a moment, his gaze traveling across my crew cut hair, pug nose, and thick jaw. He must have liked what he saw, because he opened the car door and slid out.

I'd had the chance to examine him as well. Naturally thin and wearing tight-fitting clothes that accentuated his figure, Billy was clearly a lover and not a fighter. He had alabaster skin, emerald green eyes, and finger-long blond hair matted with blood. His wounds were superficial, but even small scalp abrasions bleed like a geyser. Guys like Mulligan knew that; guys like Billy didn't.

We walked around the building, through the lobby past a security guard who'd fallen asleep at his station, to the elevators. We rode sixteen flights to my office suite, and Billy stifled a laugh when he saw the company name etched in gold leaf on the glass door:

Daniel Daqvic—Private Investigations

"You're a dick?"

"Private investigator," I corrected.

After unlocking the door and flipping on the lights, I led Billy inside. I'd done well for myself after taking early retirement from the police force, and my firm had grown to include a receptionist and two other investigators. I'd even had the place professionally decorated so that my well-heeled clients felt comfortable visiting my offices.

"My office is back here."

I'd taken the corner office for myself because it offered a panoramic view of downtown. The furnishings included a large oak desk, a leather couch, and a pair of chairs. The decorator I'd hired had kept the decor tasteful and minimal. As I led Billy into my office, I heard his breath catch.

He circumnavigated the room, examining the paintings, the ceramic figurines, and the view. Then he turned his attention to my desk.

The broad expanse of oak was empty save for my appointment book, a couple of pens, and a picture of my sister with her two children. Billy carefully examined the photograph. "You married?"

I shrugged.

"So, what were you doing at Chartreuse?"

"Coincidence," I lied. "I was working a divorce case three blocks over and was on my way back to the office when I saw you walk into the alley with Mulligan. I knew that couldn't be a good thing."

Billy considered my answer for a moment and then excused himself to use the shower in my executive washroom. While my guest cleaned himself up, I keyed a switch under my desk and then I splashed three fingers of scotch into a pair of tumblers. I emptied mine in a single gulp.

A few minutes later, Billy stepped out of the executive washroom wearing my thick, white terry-cloth bathrobe. He'd finger-combed his wet hair, and he'd obviously spritzed himself with my cologne.

I handed him a tumbler.

Billy sipped the scotch cautiously, smiled, and then sipped again. "You have good taste."

We stood so close I could feel the heat radiating from his young body. I lifted my free hand and brushed a damp lock of hair behind his ear. "I hope so."

Billy stared into my eyes without blinking. His voice was barely a whisper when he said, "I haven't properly thanked you for coming to my rescue."

My fingers were still entwined in his hair, and I held the back of his head as I leaned forward to cover his mouth with mine. When his lips parted, I thrust my tongue between them and tasted toothpaste and scotch. My cock began to swell with desire.

When our kiss ended, I loosened the sash and Billy's robe fell open, revealing his smooth chest, tight abdomen, and the neatly trimmed blond nest cradling his flaccid cock and heavy ball sac. Billy shook the robe off his shoulders, and it slid down his arms, pooling at his feet. He grasped my package through the thin material of my pants. "What about your wife?"

I turned the photograph of my sister facedown on my desk. "She won't see a thing."

Billy placed his unfinished tumbler of scotch next to the photograph, and then he dropped to his knees in front of me. By the time Billy had my pants unzipped and his hand inside my shorts, my cock was rock-hard. He freed it from the confines of my boxers and glanced up at me.

"You've got a nice dick for a dick," he said, amused by his own wordplay.

I wasn't amused by it. I wanted the young man to quit stalling and to properly show me his appreciation.

After hesitating for a moment, Billy finally leaned forward. His breath warmed the swollen purple head of my cock, and he wrapped his lips around it. His teeth caught behind the thick ridge of my glans, and he spanked my cock head with his tongue, licking away drops of pre-come. A moment later he pushed forward, taking a third of my cock into his mouth before pulling back. He did it a second time, and then a third, and each time Billy pushed his face forward, another inch of my cock disappeared into his mouth.

Then he reached around and grabbed my ass, pulling my hips forward as he pressed his face into my crotch. My entire length disappeared into the young man's oral cavity, and I gasped with surprise. Few men can take me all the way without gagging.

I wrapped my hands around the back of Billy's head, not particularly concerned if I aggravated the abrasions he'd suffered earlier, and snaked my fingers through his hair. I pulled my hips back and pushed forward, face-fucking the young blond until I couldn't hold back any longer.

I came, firing thick gobs of hot spunk against the back of Billy's throat. He quickly swallowed every drop, and then he licked my cock clean and stuffed it in my pants.

When he finished, Billy sat back on his heels and looked up at me. My zipper had scratched his chin and my belt buckle had scraped his forehead, but I don't think he realized it. I held out my hand and helped him to his feet.

While I peeled off my jacket and unfastened my shoulder rig, draping them over one of the chairs, Billy finished the last of his scotch. He watched attentively as I slipped out of the rest of my clothes and then fished through my desk drawer for a lubricated condom. When I found one, I tossed the square foil package on the desk.

Billy picked up the condom and tore it open with his teeth while I walked around the desk.

We kissed and I tasted scotch, come, and condom lubrication on Billy's lips. By then, my cock had grown hard again, and so had Billy's. His cock was smaller than mine and, while mine pointed almost straight ahead when it was fully erect, his curved upward. He slipped the condom on over my rigid rod and then he turned and bent forward over my desk, facing the windows.

I reached between his creamy alabaster thighs and fondled his heavy nut sac, rolling his nuts between my fingers and massaging them roughly. He moaned with pleasure and squirmed against the desktop. While I played with his ball sac, I used my thumb to stroke the sensitive spot between his balls and his ass hole.

When he moaned even louder, I knew he was ready. I grabbed Billy's slender hips and slipped my cock into the cleft of his ass cheeks.

"Don't tease me," Billy whispered hoarsely. "Take me now."

I pulled back, positioned the head of my cock against the tight pucker of Billy's ass, and entered him, slowly but surely, until the entire length of my cock was buried in his ass.

He was tight, almost virginal, and I held on firmly as I took him. We went at it hard and fast, my heavy balls slapping skin in time to my powerful thrusts.

I watched our translucent reflection in my office window. Beyond the glass the lights of the city spread out below us. Billy wasn't the first young man I'd had spread over my desk, and he wouldn't be the last, but the intense look of pleasure on his face made rescuing him earlier that evening that much sweeter.

When I realized Billy's emerald green eyes were open, I wondered if he was watching our reflection or enjoying the sight of the city at night. But I didn't ask. My breath began to quicken, and I pumped harder and faster. Soon I exploded into the condom.

I was breathless when I stepped back, freeing my cock

from Billy's ass. Billy straightened and turned, and I could see that he had ejaculated onto my desk, leaving the highly polished oak covered with his spunk.

After I caught my breath, I found another condom and we fucked again, this time on the couch, and then we showered together.

Afterward, I phoned for a cab and then escorted Billy downstairs past the still-sleeping guard. The cab was waiting outside, and I opened the cab door for Billy. He turned and asked, "Will I ever see you again?"

"Not likely," I told him, "but I'll probably see you again soon."

Billy hesitated a moment, but I didn't elaborate. After he slipped into the cab, I reached across the back seat and handed the driver a pair of twenties. "Take the kid wherever he wants to go."

Half an hour later, I pushed open my bedroom door and found Mulligan waiting, reading glasses perched on the end of his nose and a paperback open in his lap. He looked up. "How was he?"

"Perfect." I smiled. "They're always so grateful to be rescued."

Mulligan closed his book and placed it on the nightstand. His glasses followed a moment later. Then he flipped back the covers and patted the bed beside him. "Come tell me all about it."

"Even better," I said as I tossed a videocassette onto the bed. "I'll show you."

LIPSTICK IN THE RAIN

A single taillight winked at me as a black Taurus stopped for a red light just south of the farm supply store on the edge of town. When the traffic signal turned green, I flipped on my lightbar, and the driver of the Taurus eased his vehicle to the grassy shoulder on the far side of the intersection.

I stopped my patrol car behind the Taurus, ran wants and warrants on the license number, and waited until it came back clean before stepping into the rain. The nearest streetlamp was a block away and the quarter moon was barely visible through the clouds. The only illumination came from our headlights and the blue and red lightbar flashing on top of my patrol car. I approached the Taurus cautiously, ascertaining that the driver was alone before rapping on his window with my flashlight.

He rolled down the window and looked up at me with pale blue eyes.

I flashed the light in his face. "License, registration, and proof of insurance."

He had all three ready, and he handed them to me

through the open window. I shined the flashlight at the license, then at the driver, and then back at the license. Except for the cherry red lipstick smeared crudely across the driver's lips, the streaks of mascara down his cheeks, the tattered designer dress, and the ratty blond wig, the photograph matched the person.

"Costume party," he explained, even though I didn't ask. "Famous singers."

I shined the light in his face again. "Who the hell are you supposed to be?"

"Courtney Love."

"Have you been drinking?"

"No, sir," he said. His eyes were clear and so was his speech.

I gave the vehicle's interior a once-over with my flashlight, seeing a large black purse and a pair of stiletto heels on the passenger side floorboard. When I finished, I said, "Wait in your vehicle."

After returning to my patrol car, I called in Lee Anthony's name and driver's license number. Again, no wants or warrants. I returned to his vehicle. He'd rolled up his window to keep out the rain, so I rapped on it again.

As soon as he had the window open, I asked, "Do you know why I pulled you over, Mr. Anthony?"

"No, officer," he said. He had taken off the wig to reveal his own blond hair and the wig lay on the seat beside him. "I don't."

"One of your taillights is busted."

"Which one?"

His door opened suddenly, and I jumped back. My

revolver had cleared leather before he could swing his legs out, and his eyes widened in surprise when he saw that I had drawn on him.

"You don't want to make sudden moves, Mr. Anthony," I told him. "That's how people get shot."

He remained nearly motionless, his chest the only thing moving as his breath quickened.

The side of the dress was split nearly to his waist and I could see the full extent of one clean-shaven, muscular thigh and one tight butt cheek. I hadn't been with a man in three months and my cock twitched at the sight.

"You wearing anything under that dress?"

"Only my birthday suit," Lee responded. "I didn't want panty lines."

"Ease out of the vehicle slowly, Mr. Anthony," I instructed. "Then turn and place your hands on top of the vehicle and spread your legs."

As soon as Lee did as I instructed, I holstered my weapon and patted him down, paying special attention to his inner thighs and groin. He obviously appreciated the attention and soon the front of his dress bulged in an unfeminine way.

My own cock had tightened my uniform pants, so I grabbed my package to adjust everything before I told Lee he could straighten up and turn around. By then, the rain had petered out, leaving a faint mist hanging in the night air.

"It's the driver's side." I showed him the busted taillight.

Lee looked at the shattered red plastic for a moment and then turned to me.

"This must have happened while I was at the party," he explained. He touched my forearm with the tips of his fingers and an erotic tingle shot directly to my balls. They tightened inside my boxers. "Are you giving me a ticket?"

I made a decision I knew I might regret, but I handed him his driver's license, registration, and proof of insurance. "Not this time."

"How can I ever thank you?" Lee asked. His fingertips slowly trailed down my arm, causing my stiffening cock to throb with desire.

The town that employs me is too small and too cheap to have video cameras in the patrol cars, so I knew nothing I said or did would be seen by the department or show up on Spike TV. Even so, I didn't respond to his question immediately. I was too busy trying to figure his angle.

Lee stepped closer and his hand found my crotch, warming my package through the material of my uniform.

"Officer," he said huskily, "I think I found your baton."

I grabbed Lee's wrist and pulled him around to the other side of his vehicle, away from the road. When I unzipped my uniform pants, Lee didn't waste any time unthreading my erect cock from my boxers and pulling it out through my open fly.

He grabbed my cock like a joystick and swiped the ball of his thumb across the glistening drop of pre-come on my cock head. Then he lifted his thumb to his mouth and tasted it.

A wicked little grin split his face in two before he lifted his dress to mid-thigh and dropped to his knees in the wet grass. He wrapped one hand around my thick cock and held it as he took the spongy soft mushroom cap into his mouth. Then he spanked my cock with his tongue and massaged my balls with his free hand.

I grabbed the back of his head and pushed my cock deep into Lee's mouth. He accepted every inch before I pulled back and did it again. After the second time, he stopped me, pulling his face away. Cold mist clung to my saliva-slick cock, and it throbbed with desire.

"I want you to fuck me," Lee said as he stood. "Fuck me hard."

I glanced both ways, but there was no traffic in sight.

Lee bent over the Taurus, and I lifted the evening dress over his hips. His ass was as smooth as his legs and my cock easily nestled between his firm cheeks. I pressed forward, easing my cock into his ass. Then I grabbed his hips and fucked him hard and fast, my holster and my handcuffs rattling at my hips as I pounded into the smaller man.

He moaned with pleasure, accepting each of my thrusts by pushing his hips back toward me. He had one hand captured under the dress and I knew he was pleasuring himself as I fucked him.

When I came, I came hard, firing a thick wad of hot spunk deep inside Lee's ass. Then I held him tight until my cock finally stopped spasming and began to soften. I pulled out of Lee and stepped back, quickly stuffing my cock back into my boxers and zipping up my uniform pants.

Lee turned around and stretched up to give me a quick peck on the cheek. "I wish we had more time," he whispered hoarsely. "There's so much we could do. I could show you things you haven't even imagined."

"I've seen enough," I said. I'd probably seen too much.

Lee returned to his vehicle and a moment later the Taurus pulled onto the road. I sat in my patrol car and watched Lee drive away until I could no longer see his taillight in the distance. Then I switched off the lightbar, dropped the vehicle into gear, and turned around to cruise back through town.

I couldn't stop thinking about Lee and what we might have done if I hadn't been on the clock, and he hadn't been anxious to leave. As a small-town Texas cop, I rarely had the opportunity to meet men like Lee, and I'd had to settle for the occasional weekend trip to Austin or Houston to satisfy my needs.

Thirty minutes after parting company with Lee, I cruised past the all-night convenience store on the north end of town. I glanced in the window, and even though the place was lit up like electricity was free, I didn't see anyone working behind the counter. I pulled in, parked, and went inside. When I saw the cash register standing open and no one responded to my repeated calls, I searched the building.

I found Mr. Hamish and his adult daughter duct-taped together in the storage room. They both yelled when I pulled the tape off their mouths.

"We were robbed," Mr. Hamish said, "by a woman."

"That wasn't a woman," his daughter said. "That was a man dressed as a woman."

"It was a woman," Mr. Hamish insisted. "You think I don't know a woman when I see one?"

"What did she look like?"

He described Lee Anthony in drag.

"How much did she get?"

"Not she," his daughter insisted. "He!"

"We had almost a thousand in the cash register," Mr. Hamish said. "She got it all."

I followed him to the front counter.

"Why so much?"

"It's payday at the plant. Some of the men from third shift come here in the morning to cash their checks. We—"

My mind spun out of control. "Did you see what she was driving?"

"I didn't even see her pull in. Suddenly, there she was waving a gun in my face."

I turned to Hamish's daughter. "You?"

She shook her head. "We were caught by surprise."

As they told the story, Lee had appeared suddenly, made them open the cash register and empty the contents into a large black purse, and then had pushed them into the back room and secured them with duct tape. The entire thing hadn't taken more than five minutes.

After giving the area behind the counter a quick once-over and seeing nothing of interest, I walked outside. Around the side of the building, I found shards of red plastic next to the corner of the Dumpster Lee had backed into in his haste. By then the rain had returned.

I scraped up the pieces of Lee's taillight and dropped them into the Dumpster where no one else would look. As I walked around the building to the front door, I saw my reflection in the glass, and I saw a tiny smear of cherry red lipstick on my cheek.

While dawn peeked over the horizon, I considered everything that had happened that night, how my dick had led me astray, how Lee had been armed but had chosen a different weapon, and how I couldn't tell anyone what had happened beside the road south of town because I would lose my job.

But I had Lee's name, I had Lee's address, and I knew the next time we met one of us would get fucked. I smiled at the thought, and then I silently wiped off his lipstick in the rain.

IN THE CLOSET

When I heard the apartment door open, I stopped cold. Christopher Melon had returned home earlier than usual, and the sound of two male voices entering the apartment told me he wasn't alone. I stood in his master bedroom dressed all in black, a thick wad of his cash in one pocket, several expensive pieces of his jewelry in another.

The apartment had two exits—the door from the hallway through which Christopher and his guest had entered and the sliding glass door leading to the balcony through which I had entered twenty minutes earlier. The only path to either exit was through the living room where, from the sound of things, Christopher was preparing drinks at the wet bar.

My pulse raced and I struggled to keep my breathing steady. I had never before been trapped in a residence I was burglarizing. The closest I had ever come was more than a decade earlier, when I'd been younger and less cautious. I'd slipped out the back door of a Tudor in the Heights just as the homeowners entered through the front.

I ventured a glance into the living room. Slim,

dishwater-blond, impeccably groomed Christopher stood with his back to me. His guest, a slightly older, dark-haired man with broad shoulders and thick arms barely contained by the sleeves of his Polo shirt, stood staring into Christopher's eyes. Both held drinks.

Christopher was a regular at the Cock and Bull, one of several establishments I frequented in search of appropriate marks, but his guest was unfamiliar. When the older man wet his lips with the tip of his tongue and ran the backs of his fingers down Christopher's cheek, I knew I didn't have much time. Christopher immediately placed his unfinished drink on an end table, took his guest's hand and turned in my direction. As they approached the bedroom I backed away from the door and slipped into the walk-in closet. I left the door open a fraction of an inch so I could peek through the crack and see what was happening.

The two men didn't waste any time. They barely made it into the bedroom before the bigger man pushed Christopher against the wall only inches from the closet door. He covered Christopher's mouth with his, and one hand groped the smaller man's crotch. Christopher's slender hands fumbled with the bigger man's belt, button and zipper and soon freed his long, thick-shafted erection.

They spun around so that the dark-haired man's back was against the wall and Christopher dropped to his knees on the carpet before him. He wrapped both hands around the thick cock jutting in front of his face and took the spongy soft mushroom cap into his mouth. He licked, he sucked and then he drew in another inch of the bigger man's shaft.

That wasn't enough for the bigger man. He grabbed the back of Christopher's head and thrust his hips forward, sinking the entire length of his cock into Christopher's oral cavity. I expected Christopher to gag, but he didn't, unexpectedly impressing me. Then the bigger man drew his hips back until just his cock head remained in Christopher's mouth before he pushed forward again. His heavy ball sac bounced off Christopher's chin, and he did it again and again.

As I watched the dark-haired man face-fuck Christopher so close to me I could have reached out of the closet and touched them, my cock began to thicken and rise. I carefully shifted position to untangle it from my briefs.

The bigger man's hips began pumping faster and then he suddenly stopped with his cock buried deep inside Christopher's mouth. I watched Christopher's Adam's apple bob up and down as he swallowed wad after wad of the bigger man's come, and I swallowed hard, too, because I almost came in my shorts.

When Christopher finally pulled away, a thin string of come stretched from his lips to the bigger man's rapidly deflating cock until it finally snapped as Christopher stood.

The two men stepped away from the wall and out of my line of sight until I realized I could see the entire bedroom reflected in the mirror hung above the dresser. I watched as they stripped off their clothes. Christopher had the light, all-over tan of someone who spent time in a tanning booth. Though his face, neck and arms were the leather-brown of someone who spent a lot of time outdoors, Christopher's guest was eggshell white beneath his clothes, his only color provided by a light dusting of black body hair.

By the time they finished removing their clothes, the dark-haired man's cock had begun to resume its former stature. Christopher reached into his nightstand and retrieved a partially used tube of lube. He handed it to his guest and then lay back on the bed. His guest lay beside him and opened the tube. After he slathered lube between Christopher's ass cheeks and on his own thick cock, he lifted the slender blond's legs and nearly folded Christopher in half. Then he pressed his cock head against Christopher's lube-slathered sphincter and pressed forward until he buried his cock deep inside Christopher's ass.

Christopher's cock was trapped between them and, as the bigger man drew back and pressed forward, his abdomen rubbed against the underside of Christopher's stiff shaft.

Christopher came first, covering them with his sticky effluent. Then his guest made one final deep thrust and he came, emptying himself within Christopher.

I was so excited I felt my underwear dampen with pre-come, and it took tremendous willpower not to pull my cock out and stroke it into submission. I didn't dare though. I knew that getting caught in a man's closet with his valuables in my pockets was bad but getting caught in his closet with my hand wrapped around my valuables was infinitely worse. So, my erection and I waited patiently while the two men snuggled, fucked yet again and then snuggled more.

I waited a long time in that closet, until I was certain, from the sound of their breathing, that both men were asleep. Then I slipped from the bedroom, across the living room, out through the sliding glass door, and over the rail to the ground one floor below. My nondescript car, parked two blocks away, remained undisturbed.

Once home, I sat on the toilet, took my still-hard cock in my hand, and churned butter until I came with a rush that painted the back of the bathroom door with come before I could catch it in the tissue I held in my free hand.

The next day I fenced Christopher's jewelry, more valuable for its gold content than its craftsmanship, and pocketed the cash. That evening I took myself out for a steak dinner accompanied by a moderately priced bottle of wine and flirted with my handsome waiter. Tony had waited on me several times over the years I'd been dining at Carvello's but was half of a committed relationship and had long ago made it clear that nothing would ever come of my flirtation.

Then I relaxed that evening at Leon's, a dark neighborhood bar where I could enjoy myself without thinking about work. Other evenings in other bars led to other apartments and other homes. As nondescript as my car, I watched the pickups and kiss-offs, learning the routines of potential marks. I paid attention to who went home early and who remained until closing, who left alone and who left on the arm of another man, and who actually had money and who merely fronted. I followed the best marks, learned where they lived, and determined whose homes were easily accessible and whose were best avoided. Then, when I felt confident that I would have sufficient uninterrupted time, I visited some of those homes, leaving with hundreds and sometimes thousands of dollars worth of cash and easily fenced valuables.

And every time I was inside one of those homes without an invitation, I thought about what I'd seen in Christopher Melon's apartment. I'd never thought of myself as the type of guy who liked to watch other men having sex—I hadn't even watched porn since dropping out of junior college—but I frequently found myself churning butter while mentally replaying that scene.

I worked a circuit, never too many consecutive nights spent at the same bar, never at the same bar so often that bartenders and barflies recognized me, but often enough that I knew the routines of their most affluent regulars. Then one night I found myself back at the Cock and Bull, Christopher Melon's favorite watering hole, and he was there, leaning against the bar, waiting to be approached. My cock twitched at the memory of Christopher giving his dark-haired guest a blow job only inches from me.

I plied Christopher with drinks, maybe even using his own money, and soon felt his hand between my thighs, cupping my balls and squeezing my tumescent cock through the material of my chinos. I already knew what he looked like naked, what he looked like with a cock in his mouth, and what he looked like in the throes of passion. What I didn't know, until that moment, is what he felt like, and I liked the way my cock felt in his hand, even with layers of cloth between them. I watched his reflection in the mirror behind the bar, much like I had watched his reflection that night in his bedroom, and I suggested there might be somewhere private we could go.

Christopher removed his hand from my crotch, finished his drink and took me back to his apartment. Once inside he offered me a drink, apparently following some long-established script of seduction.

I declined the drink, took his hand and led him to his bedroom.

"You act like you've been here before," he said.

I didn't say anything. Instead, I opened the closet door and looked inside.

"What are you doing?" he asked.

"Humor me," I said. "This will just take a moment."

I enjoyed watching but I wouldn't enjoy being watched. I switched on the light, saw nothing but clothing and shoes, and switched it off again.

Then I turned to Christopher, pulled him into my arms, and covered his mouth with mine. We kissed long, deep and hard before I peeled off his clothes and fucked him until he screamed with pleasure.

DICKED

I was sitting at the hotel bar nursing my second Jack-and-Coke when a man straddled the empty stool to my left and unbuttoned his jacket. I examined his reflection in the mirror as he caught the bartender's attention and ordered a gimlet with a twist. He wore a navy-blue two-piece suit over a crisp white shirt, a rep tie still firmly knotted at the collar. Finger-length black hair lightly frosted with silver had been parted on the left with laser-like precision and a day's growth of beard shadowed his square jaw. His hands were free of jewelry, but a gold Rolex peeked out from his left shirt cuff.

The bartender presented the man's gimlet and then faded away to attend to a portly gentleman in an ill-fitting brown suit sitting at the opposite end of the bar. Several stools remained empty between the portly gentleman and me, and my new companion could have settled onto any of them.

"Long day?" I asked without turning. I had blown off two other men before his arrival.

He eyed my reflection and then turned to face me.

"Long enough," he said, but the way he said it let me know he wasn't talking about his day. "Yours?"

"The same."

He smiled. As he turned to face me, his jacket opened for a moment. I caught a glimpse of his shoulder holster and the .38 tucked into it, and I marveled at the skill of his tailor. If I hadn't known to look for his sidearm, I might never have suspected it was there because the cut of his jacket completely disguised its presence. I wondered which pocket held the leather wallet containing his badge and I.D.

As he rested his hand on my thigh, he said, "I haven't seen you here before."

"It's my first time," I said. "A friend suggested this place."

"Your friend's stayed here?"

"He said it was the best place in Dallas to meet like-minded men of discretion."

"It certainly is," my new companion said. He sipped from his gimlet. "Where are you from?"

"St. Louis," I lied. "I'm traveling on business."

He nodded at the ring on my left hand. "Married?"

I lied again, feeding him exactly the information he needed to hear. "Wife, two kids, house in the suburbs."

He finished his drink and caught the bartender's eye. "Another of these," he said as he touched his glass, "and another for my new friend."

My third Jack-and-Coke was as weak as the first two, an arrangement I'd made with the bartender when I'd placed my first order.

As my new friend and I sipped our drinks, his hand inched up my thigh to the bulge at my crotch, and we continued our small talk as if nothing unusual were happening. I continued feeding him the lies he needed to hear and, after he finished his second gimlet, I suggested we finish our conversation in my room.

His eyes narrowed as he examined me. For a moment I thought I'd been too forward and was afraid that I had aroused his suspicion, but he squeezed my thigh and said, "I think I'm up for that."

My suite on the top floor was part of the lie, implying a disposable income I didn't posses, and he was suitably impressed when I pushed the door open and turned on the light.

In the privacy of my suite, he became less refined and less reserved. "Why don't you take off those clothes and show me what you've got?"

I matched his crudity. "I need to take a leak first."

"You do that."

While I was in the bathroom, he opened the minibar without asking and fixed himself a drink. He was finishing it when I returned wearing one of the complementary bathrobes I'd found hanging in the bedroom closet.

He'd used the time I was out of sight to remove his jacket and shoulder holster, and he'd neatly hidden his sidearm beneath his jacket when he'd draped it over the back of the couch, much as I'd hidden the wire I'd been wearing.

He grabbed hold of the sash keeping my robe closed and unthreaded it. The robe parted, revealing my nudity beneath. He must have liked what he saw because he pushed the robe off my shoulders and watched as it slithered down my arms and fell to the floor at my feet.

Then he grabbed my jaw in one meaty fist, tilted my head back, and kissed me deep and hard.

"You came all the way to Dallas for this, didn't you?"

This time I didn't have to lie. "Yes," I said. "Yes, I did."

My friend had told me exactly what to expect from the cop who held my jaw, from the approach at the bar to the rough sex to the post-sex shakedown. What I didn't know is if he would give me the same name he'd given my friend. "You got a name?"

"Does it matter?"

"I need to call you something."

"Call me Dick," he said, with the same lack of originality he'd displayed seven months earlier.

"Okay, Dick," I said as I slipped one hand under his belt and into his boxers, answering my question even as I asked it. "You ready to do this?"

His thick cock throbbed in my hand as I wrapped my fist around it, and I felt a slick drop of pre-come tickle my wrist. I used my free hand to unbuckle his belt and unzip his slacks. As his pants dropped to the floor, he pushed my shoulders down until I knelt on the floor in front of him.

I peeled his boxers out of the way and took the head of his cock between my teeth. That wasn't enough for Dick, and he pressed against the back of my head until I took his entire length into my oral cavity. The unkempt black nest of his pubic hair tickled my nostrils and made me want to sneeze.

Dick held my head between his hands as he drew his hips back and pushed forward, slamming his cock head against the back of my throat and bouncing his heavy balls off my chin. While his cock was thick, it wasn't long enough to make me gag, and I easily accepted every one of his thrusts. I grabbed his ass cheeks and held tight, digging my nails into the firm flesh and leaving tiny half-moon indentions as I scraped a bit of his skin under my fingernails.

His ball sac began to tighten and his hips began moving faster, so I was prepared when Dick suddenly stopped and fired a thick wad of hot spunk against the back of my throat. I swallowed and swallowed again, and when his cock finally stopped spasming in my mouth, Dick released his grip on my head.

I pulled away and sat back on my heels. My cock stood erect, straining for attention I knew he wouldn't provide, so I wrapped my fist around it and jerked off while Dick undressed. A good-looking man, stocky without being fat, he was the type of guy I would have invited into my bed even under other circumstances. As it was, I was enjoying myself more than he could have ever imagined.

Dick had removed all his clothes and placed them with his jacket before I came, and I shot a thin stream of come across the carpet that almost reached the couch where he'd placed them. He saw what was happening and said, "Hey, watch the clothes. I have places to be later. I don't want to have to go home and change."

I still had my hand wrapped around my cock when Dick hooked a hand under my arm and pulled me to my feet. His cock had begun to regain its former stature.

"You got lube?"

"In the bedroom."

He propelled me in that direction, through the doorway toward the king-size bed. An unopened tube of lube lay on the nightstand, and he grabbed it. He opened it, slathered some on his cock, and then spun me around and pushed me facedown on the bed. He grabbed my hips and pulled upward until I realized what he was doing and drew my knees under me so that my ass stuck up in the air.

Dick slathered lube into the crack of my ass, massaged it into my ass hole until he could slip one and then two fingers into me. He used far more lube than necessary, and it dripped down the underside of my ball sac onto the bed. A moment later he withdrew his fingers and pressed his cock head against my slick sphincter. He grabbed my hips and thrust forward, driving his cock deep into me.

Even though I'd been expecting it, I still wasn't quite prepared for how rough he was. His grip was so tight he bruised my hips as he drew back and slammed forward, his lube-slick cock sliding in and out of me faster and harder.

My cock grew hard as Dick fucked me, and I was so turned on I almost forgot why I was there. I reached between my thighs and caught some of the lube dripping from my ball sac. Then I wrapped my fist around my cock and pumped in counter-rhythm to Dick's ever-quickening thrusts.

He came first, with one last powerful thrust that almost drove me off my knees. I only remained as I was because of his powerful grip. As he fired hot spunk into me, I continued pumping my fist until I came, sending my own wad of spunk onto the bedspread beneath me.

Dick held me until his cock stopped spasming, and then he stepped back, releasing his grip on me as he pulled away. I collapsed on the bed, lying on my own wet spot, but I didn't care.

I rolled over and looked at him.

"Worth the trip?" he asked.

"So far," I said with a smile.

"You think you can do this again?" he asked with a smirk.

I knew one of us would get fucked again before he left, but I shook my head.

He stepped into the bathroom and left the door open while he urinated and washed his crotch. Then he walked into the other room, and I watched through the open door as he dressed.

I knew just the question to ask when he lifted his jacket off the back of the couch and revealed his shoulder holster. "Why do you have a gun?"

He strapped on the holster, slipped on his jacket and returned to the bedroom. He retrieved a worn brown wallet from his hip pocket. He flipped it open to reveal his badge and I.D. "Because I'm a cop."

"A cop?"

"And soliciting's a crime." He returned the wallet to his hip pocket.

I feigned befuddlement. "Soliciting?"

"You approached me in the bar, invited me to your room, and offered sex for money."

"I did?"

"Be a shame if your wife got word of this." He stepped into the bathroom, found my clothes, and dug through my pants for my wallet. He opened it, thumbed out the driver's license, and added, "Doug."

I understood how he had been able to intimidate my friend. "But I didn't do what you said I did."

"A real shame, Doug," he continued. "What about your employer? Think they'd be interested in knowing what you do when they send you out of town?"

"I—I—" I stuttered. "What can I do to make this go away?"

"Are you offering to bribe me, Doug?"

"No, I—I just—"

He smiled. "A thousand dollars. This could all disappear for a thousand dollars."

"I—I don't have that much money with me."

Dick looked in my wallet. "I can see that." He thumbed out the cash, counted it, and said, "One-eighty-seven is a good start."

"But—"

"That's okay," he said as he pocketed the cash and thumbed out my debit card. "There's an ATM in the lobby."

"I have a two hundred a day limit."

He thumbed out my credit cards. "Cash advances on these'll make up the difference."

The time had come to turn the tables. "And if I don't pay you, you'll tell my wife and my employer?"

"I thought that was obvious."

"So, you're shaking me down."

He shrugged. "Call it what you will."

I reached for the remote and switched on the television. An image of the two of us sitting at the bar downstairs filled the screen.

"I think I'd call it early retirement, *Dick*." I folded my hands behind my head. "You turn in your badge or copies of this tape get sent to Internal Affairs, the DA's office, and—"

His smirk disappeared. He interrupted me by reaching under his jacket and removing his .38. "You son-of-a—"

"I wouldn't if I were you." I pointed at the television. Seven months earlier Dick had shaken down my friend and now my friend sat in the next suite watching and recording everything as it happened. The scene on the television screen switched from the recording of Dick and me in the bar to a live feed of Dick pointing his .38 at me.

I watched my cock get hard and said, "It looks like you're getting fucked this time."

DO THE HUSTLE

I quietly removed all the cash from the wallet of the corpulent man snoring on the queen bed, adding $237 to the $100 he'd given me earlier in the evening. I knew he would notice the lightness of his wallet when he awoke the next morning, but I felt confident he would not report his loss to the police because to do so would implicate him in an illegal act, and the news would certainly get back to his family, friends, and employer in whatever small town had regurgitated him a few days earlier. I stuffed the money in my pocket and let myself out of the hotel room.

Thirty minutes later I bellied up to the bar at The Butt Inn, ordered a rum-and-Coke, and paid for it with money I had taken from the John. Henry was working the stick that night and his mixed drinks always contained a generous pour of the off-brand liquor his employer made him serve. I knocked back half the drink in one quick swallow, knowing the cheap liquor would kill the taste in my mouth.

"What happened to that guy you left with earlier?" Henry asked.

"You know men," I replied. "They come and they go."

"Or they come and you go."

We both laughed.

The older man knew me well. I had been using The Butt Inn to pick up Johns for several years because it was in the heart of the hotel district and catered to business travelers directed to the bar by concierges with greased palms.

"It's still early," he said. "Are you looking for a little more action tonight?"

The fat guy had only wanted a blowjob so I felt confident that I could be up for anything. "Sure."

Henry nodded toward the back. "Light beer in the back booth is cruising but he's trying not to be obvious."

I glanced over my shoulder, but I couldn't see into the booth from where I sat. I caught a glimpse of a jacket sleeve with a French cuff and a large left hand protruding from it, indicating that the man was keeping his back to the bar. Neon light from a nearby beer sign reflected from the chunky gold wedding ring adorning the hand.

I knocked back the last of my drink and pushed the empty glass across the bar.

"He running a tab?"

Henry nodded.

"Set us up when I get back."

The Butt Inn had been my first stop after leaving the corpulent man at the hotel, so I needed to clean up before approaching the gentleman in the back booth. I slipped off the barstool and made my way down the hall to the men's room, where I found mouthwash and a selection of cologne. The bar's owner was stingy with his liquor, but he knew exactly what amenities kept his customers coming back.

After gargling with the mouthwash, I spritzed on some cheap cologne that didn't clash with the more expensive cologne I had applied before leaving my apartment early that evening. I combed my hair, made certain my shirt was tucked in and my jacket collar lay flat, and gave my reflection the once over. When I was satisfied, I headed back to the bar.

I stopped at the entrance to the hall and examined the man sitting in the back booth—mid-40s, graying at the temples, and far too well dressed for The Butt Inn. He examined me in return, apparently liked what he saw, and nodded.

I slipped into the booth and sat facing him across the table. Before either of us spoke, Henry arrived with the drinks I had ordered.

"I didn't—"

"I did," I told my companion as Henry walked away. Henry would add the drinks and a healthy tip to my companion's tab, but the sucker wouldn't realize it until he received his credit card statement, a scam Henry and I had pulled many times before.

My companion pushed his empty bottle aside and lifted the fresh one to his lips. After he took a small sip, he then placed the bottle on the table between us. I had one hand wrapped around my rum-and-Coke, but I had yet to take a drink.

"To what do I owe the pleasure of your company and your generosity?" he asked.

"Henry says you're looking for companionship. Is that true?"

"I'm certainly not opposed to it."

We danced around the subject for a bit and then he told me exactly what he desired from a man of my particular persuasion.

The man sitting across from me was someone who would have caught my attention even if I were off the clock, but I had bills to pay so I named a price. When he didn't blink, I asked, "Staying nearby?"

He named a hotel less than two miles from the bar, and not the one I had been in less than an hour earlier.

"We could continue this discussion there," I suggested.

"What's your hurry?" he asked.

I took a sip from my drink. "No hurry."

"Good," he said. He lifted his beer. "You were kind enough to buy me this drink. I'd like to finish it before we go."

I didn't know why he was hesitating until I saw him pluck a pill from his shirt pocket and wash it down with a swallow of beer.

"You've done this before?" he finally asked.

"Once or twice," I admitted.

He lifted the beer bottle to his lips and took a long slow drink.

"You?" I asked.

His pale blue eyes twinkled when he replied, "Once or twice. I've gotten quite good at it."

As I sipped my rum-and-Coke, my new companion caught Henry's attention and had the bartender call a cab. We finished our drinks while awaiting its arrival, and then rode in near silence to the hotel. In the bright lights of the lobby, I had the opportunity to again appraise my companion. His tailored suit easily cost as much as I paid for a month's rent, and he carried himself in a manner that led me to believe he was accustomed to having people wait on him and getting what he wanted without hesitation.

We crossed the lobby without incident, not drawing undue attention the way some of my Johns did, and rode the elevator to the seventh floor.

I wasn't paying attention when he unlocked the door to Suite 716, so I didn't see his room key, and I saw nothing as we walked through the suite that indicated he had unpacked. I presumed his suitcase was tucked away in one of the closets, waiting untouched until he needed something from within it.

Once inside the bedroom, he removed four crisp Benjamins from the thick wad of bills in his wallet and laid them on the corner of the dresser. I scooped them up and stuffed them into my pocket.

My client settled into a chair, leaned back, and crossed his legs. "Let me see what I've paid for."

I wasn't a stripper, so I didn't bump and grind. I simply removed my jacket and laid it on the dresser where the four Benjamins had been only moments before. Then I removed my shirt by unbuttoning it slowly, pulling it free of my pants, and then shaking it off my shoulders so that it slid down my arms and dropped to the carpet at my feet. I did not wear a T-shirt because I had long ago learned the value of dressing quickly and vacating rooms in a hurry.

Though I do not sport a six-pack, I keep myself in good shape. I have broad shoulders with muscular arms, a thick chest, and a narrow waist. I don't naturally grow much chest hair, and I keep it at bay by regularly shaving my chest, just as I had that morning.

"Please continue," he said.

I wore loafers without socks, so it was easy to step out of my shoes and nudge them away with the side of my foot. I unfastened my belt, unhooked the waistband of my Chinos, and slid the zipper down. I hooked my thumbs in the waistband of my black bikini briefs and lowered them as I lowered my pants. Once my pants were pooled around my ankles, I straightened up and stepped out of them.

I am more shower than grower and my flaccid cock and heavy ball sac hung from a neatly groomed nest of blond pubic hair.

My client spun his index finger in a circle, so I turned slowly, allowing him to inspect my naked body from all sides. When I was again facing him, he nodded as if approving of the package I had unwrapped.

He stood and removed his clothes, carefully hanging his jacket on the back of the chair he had just abandoned. He placed his shoes side-by-side before the chair and carefully folded the rest of his clothing before placing it in the chair.

I admired his body as he revealed it. Though he had a

good twenty years on me and was a bit thicker around the middle, he had clearly taken care of himself, and I knew I would enjoy the coming hours.

He had told me exactly what he wanted from me while we were sitting in the booth at The Butt Inn, so I crossed the room to where he stood and dropped to my knees before him. His thick cock was but a nub before I wrapped my lips around it, and my oral attention quickly brought it life.

As his cock grew to its full length, I wrapped my fist around the thick shaft and pulled his foreskin back. I tongued his cock head, covering it completely with my saliva before slowly taking his entire length into my oral cavity. He didn't manscape as closely as I, so when I had taken in his entire length his curly black pubic hair tickled my nose and made me want to sneeze.

I quickly drew back until my teeth caught on the ridge of his swollen glans. Then I did it again. My client reached down and wrapped his hands around the back of my head. Then he held my head stationary as he pumped his hips forward and back. With each forward thrust, his heavy ball sac slapped against my chin, and each time his cock head hit the back of my throat I had to remind myself to relax.

My cock grew hard, but I did nothing about it. He wasn't paying me to please myself. I reached up and grabbed his firm ass cheeks, gripping them tightly as he face-fucked me. I knew he wouldn't last much longer when his ball sac tightened and his speed increased. I was prepared when he thrust his pelvis into my face one last time and warm come flooded my mouth. I swallowed and swallowed again as his cock spasmed within my oral cavity.

After I licked it clean, I drew back, letting his slowly deflating cock drop free of my mouth. He didn't bother helping me up. Instead, he stepped backward and sat on the edge of the bed, his legs spread wide, his semi-erect cock dangling between his thighs.

"I don't have any lube," he said, "but there's hand lotion in the bathroom."

I rose and crossed the bedroom, my erection leading the way. Inside the bathroom, I found everything the way the hotel maid had left it. My client had not yet unpacked his toiletries and he had not touched anything in the bathroom. Even the end of the toilet paper roll was still folded into a point. A moment later, I returned to the bed with a small bottle of lotion in my hand.

My client had turned down the covers and was sitting upright in the bed, leaning back against the headboard. I climbed on the bed and sat beside him. By then my erection had mostly subsided.

I looked again at the wedding band on his left hand. I didn't know if he was in the closet or not, if he was hiding his sexuality from a wife or hiding his desires for other men from a husband. I didn't often wonder why my clients chose to pay for anonymous sex. With many of them—the overweight, the ugly, and the socially inept—it was obvious. With the man sitting beside me it wasn't. He had to be getting something from our assignation that I was too blind to see.

He didn't allow me much time to think about it

because he took my hand and placed it in his lap. His cock had not gone completely flaccid, and when I touched it, it quickly returned to its former stature. I knew then that the pill he had taken at the bar was Viagra or Cialis because the refractory period for the average man his age without chemical enhancement was far longer.

I opened the bottle of lotion, slathered some on his cock, and then reached behind my ball sac to coat my ass hole with it. A moment later I lay facedown on the bed and my client was on his knees between my spread thighs. He slid one finger down the crack of my lotion-slickened ass until he found the tight pucker of my ass hole.

He pressed the tip of his finger against my ass hole until it finally opened to him. Slick with lotion, his finger slid in up to the second knuckle. As he pistoned his finger in and out, my cock began to grow hard again, and I shifted position on the bed so that it was trapped beneath my abdomen.

He eased a second finger into my ass and quickly withdrew it. Then he lay atop me, pressed the head of his cock where his fingers had just been, and drove his cock deep into me.

He drew back and pressed forward, fucking me hard and fast. The mattress bucked beneath us, and the motion of my client ramming into my ass caused my erection to rub hard against the sheet. I couldn't stop myself and I came. Warm come clung to my abdomen and practically glued it to the sheet.

The man fucking my ass paid no attention to my orgasm. He continued drilling me, slamming into me harder and harder until he cried out, stiffened, and erupted within my ass. He collapsed atop me and lay there pressing me into the mattress until his cock stopped spasming, softened, and slowly withdrew. Then he rolled to the side and lay beside me.

I ventured a question as I rolled onto my back. "You come to town often?"

"My first time," he said. "I probably won't be back."

I smiled in the darkness. Like with the fat man earlier in the evening, I had no expectation of blowback if I emptied his wallet before I slipped out of the suite.

We fucked several more times that night thanks to whatever chemical enhancement my client had taken at The Butt Inn, and I was so satiated that I did something I never do when I'm with a client.

I fell asleep.

When I awoke the next morning, I was surprised to find myself alone in the bed. I listened carefully but could hear no one moving around anywhere else in the suite. Finally, I rose from the bed and padded barefoot into the bathroom, showered, and returned to the bedroom with a towel wrapped around my waist. Only then did I realize that the man with whom I had spent the night would not be returning.

None of the towels had been disturbed until I used one. I had not seen any luggage the night before and I didn't see any now, even after opening all the closets. His clothes were gone as was every other indication that I'd had company other than the rumpled, come-stained sheets.

Something didn't seem right. I quickly pulled on my clothes and hurried from the suite, letting the door swing shut and lock behind me. I didn't bother checking my pockets until I was in the elevator descending to the lobby.

The four $100-dollar bills my companion had given me were gone, and when I opened my wallet, I discovered that all the cash I had taken from the fat man earlier that evening was gone, as was the emergency $20 I kept folded up behind my driver's license.

I stopped at the front desk and asked who had been registered in Suite 716 the previous night and what time he had checked out.

The young woman behind the desk checked her computer and told me that no one had been registered in that suite.

"That's impossible," I said. "I just came from there."

"You must be mistaken, sir," she said. "Perhaps you were in 714 or 718. Both of those were occupied last night." She glanced down at her computer screen. "Those families checked out first thing this morning."

I knew I wasn't mistaken, and I also knew not to continue drawing attention to myself. I told her that I probably was mistaken and thanked her for her assistance. Then I exited the hotel as quickly as possible and walked to the bank at the end of the block, looking for an ATM where I could get enough cash to pay for a taxi ride home.

I don't know how he had gotten it, but the man with whom I had spent the night had a hotel passkey. I also knew without talking to Henry that he had paid for our drinks at The Butt Inn with a stolen credit card, and I knew as well as he did that I could not report my loss to the police without implicating myself in an illegal act. In short, my companion the previous evening had outhustled me.

In my occupation I screw a lot of people, but this time I had been screwed.

REPRIEVE

After the sun slipped behind the high-rise horizon and the street below me became littered with neon and incandescent light, I knelt on the flat tarpaper roof of an old warehouse turned office building, leaned against the waist-high brick parapet, and peered through the scope of my high-powered rifle. My target's apartment was half a floor lower than my vantage point, at the southwest corner of a building four blocks away. I examined the interior of the apartment through the bedroom window and through the sliding glass door that separated the balcony from the living room, admiring the decorator's taste until Kevin Foreman stepped from the bathroom wearing nothing but a bulging blue jockstrap sparkling with silver glitter.

My finger tightened on the trigger. I could have taken Foreman out right then, but he suddenly grabbed a white terrycloth robe from the bed and slipped into it as he hurried from the bedroom and through the living room. He paused, tied the sash, ran his fingers through his damp blond hair to push it behind his ears, and seemed to take a deep breath to calm himself. Then he opened the apartment door and greeted the man standing on the other side. I wouldn't know what either man was saying until I had an unobstructed view of their faces and could read their lips, but I could make assumptions about them from their appearance.

The two men were quite a contrast. From what I had seen when he stepped from the bathroom and before he had pulled on the robe, Foreman had the body of a naturally slender man gone soft, neither overweight nor well toned, a light all-over tan, and he kept his face and pretty much everything else from his neck down clean-shaven. The man filling the doorway was several years older than Foreman, with a granite jaw covered by a dark, post-five-o'clock shadow, a square face the color and texture of worn leather, and closely cropped black hair sprinkled heavily with salt at the temples. He wore a navy blue, single-breasted suit jacket over his thick chest, crisp button-down white shirt, and a red tie still knotted at the neck this late in the evening. Sharply creased trousers that matched the jacket led down to black Oxfords shined to a high gloss, and the only jewelry I could see was a gold band on his left ring finger. The scar on his right cheek, the probable result of a close encounter with a knife during his youth, told me more about him than he would have expected. He was much like the men who usually hired me.

Foreman moved aside as his visitor stepped into the apartment. After my target closed and locked the door, the two men embraced. The bigger man pulled Foreman close, and when my target tilted his face upward, the bigger man covered his mouth with his own. The kiss was long and deep, and when it ended, Foreman said, "I've missed you, Domenico."

I should have packed it in right then. My plan had been to take out my target late in the evening so that I would be far away before anyone discovered his body the following day. I had not planned for, did not desire, and had been specifically instructed to avoid collateral damage. I removed my index finger from the trigger and rested it on the trigger guard, but I did not remove my eye from the scope.

Foreman splashed three fingers of Jack Daniel's into a tumbler and handed it to the big man, who knocked it back in one long swallow. He wiped his mouth with the back of his hand, a mannerism more consistent with a man of lower-class upbringing than his smartly tailored suit implied. Money had clearly not bought him class.

"Another?"

Domenico shook his head.

They spoke for a moment before Foreman untied the sash and let his terrycloth robe drape open. When Domenico saw the sparkling blue jockstrap, a smile bisected his face. Then he loosened his tie, unthreaded it from his collar, and dropped it over the back of the black leather couch. He peeled off his jacket and it joined the tie.

Foreman stepped forward to unbutton the big man's shirt, starting at the neck, and he didn't stop when he reached the bottom button. He unfastened Domenico's belt, unbuttoned his trousers, and tugged down his zipper.

He dropped to his knees, hesitated, and looked up. He said something and Domenico responded with a nod. Then Foreman reached into Domenico's trousers and pulled out a thick, semi-erect cock that was rapidly rising to its full potential. He wrapped one hand around the stiffening shaft and took the swollen purple mushroom cap into his mouth.

How I earn my living is much more than a job; it is also unexpectedly arousing. My cock was already erect from the thought of what I'd been about to do, and it throbbed as I watched one man going down on another. I had seen many things through my riflescope while I was on the job, but I had never seen anything like this. I swallowed hard and kept watching.

Foreman took the entire length of Domenico's cock into his mouth and then pulled back. He did it again and again until the bigger man's cock glistened with saliva. By then Domenico had grown impatient with Foreman's slow oral caresses. He grabbed the back of Foreman's head, wrapped his thick, sausage-like fingers in Foreman's blond hair, and held tight as he face-fucked the younger man.

Domenico suddenly stopped, the twisted expression on his face making it clear that he'd just erupted in Foreman's mouth. My target's Adam's apple bobbed up and down several times as he sought to swallow the load ejected against the back of his throat, but it was clear that he wasn't swallowing fast enough because a thin trickle of come escaped from the corner of his mouth, slid down his chin, and dripped to the carpet below.

Despite the cool evening breeze coming off the lake,

my head was sweltering inside my watch cap. I used my left hand to wipe the sweat from my forehead, unzip my leather jacket, and adjust the bulge in the crotch of my Levi's. I had traveled halfway around the world from my island home to eliminate a man with extreme prejudice and I couldn't complete the contract because he was entertaining a guest. I knew I should abort the assignment before a civilian spotted me kneeling on the roof and wondered why I was dressed entirely in black and had a high-powered rifle pointed down the block, but still I kept watching.

After Domenico helped Foreman to his feet, my target shrugged the white terrycloth robe from his shoulders and let it slide down his arms to pool on the carpet at his feet. Domenico smiled and slapped one cheek of Foreman's ass with the flat of his hand. Then he slapped the other cheek, leaving a red handprint each time. Foreman laughed and said, "Think you'll be able to do it again?"

I couldn't see Domenico's lips to know his reply, but I tracked the two men as Domenico chased my target from the living room to the bedroom, where Foreman flopped on the pastel-blue comforter and lay on his back watching Domenico. The bigger man sat heavily on the side of the bed, unlaced and removed his black Oxfords, then peeled off his black socks and tucked them into his shoes. He stood, stripped off his trousers and hung them over the back of a chair. His white dress shirt, V-neck undershirt, and baggy white BVDs followed. The heavy salt at his temples extended southward to the hair on his barrel chest, to his thick but firm abdomen, and the dense mat of his pubic hair. His thick, rapidly inflating phallus and heavy ball sac slapped his muscular thighs as he crossed the room and grabbed Foreman's ankle.

Domenico dragged the smaller man off the comforter and then spun Foreman around and bent him over the far side of the bed. With Domenico behind Foreman, I could watch both of their faces through my scope. The bigger man grabbed a tube of lube from the nightstand and squeezed a healthy dollop into Foreman's ass crack. Then he massaged it in with his thick fingers until he was able to slide one lubed finger into Foreman's sphincter. He pistoned his finger into and out of Foreman several times before replacing it with his cock. He positioned himself behind my target and pressed his cock head against the smaller man's sphincter. Then he grabbed Foreman's slim hips and held tight as he slammed forward and drove his thick cock deep into Foreman's shit chute.

Foreman's eyes widened and he bit his bottom lip as Domenico drew back and pushed forward. I could only imagine the sound of Domenico's heavy balls slapping against Foreman as he pounded into the smaller man, and I could only imagine the mewling sounds Foreman made with each of Domenico's powerful thrusts.

By then my throbbing cock was hard enough to pound nails and I had to do something to relieve the pressure. I wanted to free myself from the confines of my clothes, but I knew better. If I came on the brick parapet or the tar-paper roof, I would leave behind DNA evidence that would tie me to the scene more than any random fibers from my clothing.

I loosened my belt and removed my glove. Then I slid my left hand under the waistband of my boxers. Wishing I had lotion or lube to smooth my dry, chapped hand, I grabbed my cock and, though it was difficult to keep the rifle still while I stroked myself, continued to watch Domenico slam into my target's ass. Before long, my hand's rhythm matched the rhythm of Domenico's hips.

Domenico came first, throwing back his head and letting loose some sort of primal scream as he slammed into Foreman one last time and held the smaller man's hips in a vice grip that was certain to leave bruises.

Several strokes later, I came in my shorts, hot sticky come covering my fist as quickly as my cock spat it out. My eyelids fluttered and the rifle wavered until the orgasm passed. I pulled my hand from my boxers and wiped it on my thigh, leaving as much of the viscous fluid on the leg of my Levi's before I wedged my hand back in my glove.

I had lost track of what was happening in the apartment. So, I pressed my eye to the riflescope again and refocused on the bedroom four blocks away. Domenico was flat on his back on the bed, apparently asleep. Foreman was beside him. He had slipped out of the jockstrap, revealing a cock that easily rivaled Domenico's for length, but not for thickness. He squeezed a drop of lube into his palm and began stroking himself while staring at the sleeping bulk of his partner.

I knew I couldn't eliminate my target that night, so I let him play with himself while I broke down the rifle and returned it to the foam-padded briefcase in which I transported it. Though I had not touched anything on the roof, fibers from my clothing might have clung to the tar paper under my knees or the brick parapet I'd leaned against, but I couldn't do anything about that except burn my clothes at the first opportunity.

I policed the area as best I could, grabbed my briefcase with my dismantled rifle securely packed inside, and walked to a stairwell door I'd left unlocked. I hurried down several flights of stairs and exited the building through a side door.

As I walked to my car two blocks away, I used a disposable cell phone to dial a memorized number. When a woman answered, I said, "I was unable to complete the contract. He had company."

"I know," she said. "My husband."

With that one comment I knew my client was not a professional. I smashed the phone and threw the parts in a dumpster. I would complete the contract later. Right then I had a hard-on, knew where to find a discrete gay bar, and had the rest of the night to kill.

MAKING ROOM AT THE TOP

Little Stevie adjusted his tie and looked at his reflection in the bathroom mirror. He saw my reflection over his shoulder and smiled. I'd spent a lot of my free time behind him, and his smile grew bigger when I reached into my pants.

The smile disappeared when he saw me raise a .38, and a moment later his last thought splattered across the mirror.

"You take care of things?"

I sat with Big Tony in the back room of his restaurant, a plate of cannelloni in front of me, a half-eaten mound of linguini in clam sauce in front of him. Spots of clam sauce clung to each of his double chins.

"I changed Little Stevie's mind," I said. After I'd shot him, I'd called the cleaners, a pair of dykes who made bodies and evidence disappear. "He won't be talking to anybody."

"He give you any trouble?"

"Nothing I couldn't handle."

Big Tony belched into his fist. "Any of this going to come back on me?"

"If you thought that was a possibility," I asked, "you wouldn't have asked me to do this."

Tony glared at me, his little pig eyes black as coal. "You got chutzpah, talking to me like that."

Maybe I did. Maybe I didn't. Big Tony carried a lot of weight, but not near as much as he once had. The gentlemen I worked for tolerated Tony as long as he produced, and lately his revenue had been dropping. He'd blamed Little Stevie, claiming his debt collector had been skimming money and accepting payment in blowjobs rather than hard cash. When he'd confronted Little Stevie about it, Stevie had denied the accusations and had then made vague threats about ratting out the fat man.

Or so Big Tony claimed.

I doubted his story, but I wasn't paid to argue with the bosses, only to find permanent solutions to their problems.

"I need me somebody to work the fag bars now," Big Tony said around another mouthful of pasta. Little Stevie had worked The District for Big Tony, a part of town with a high concentration of gay-owned businesses, many of which directly and indirectly owed their existence to Big Tony's willingness to squeeze a dollar from anything or anyone that drew a breath. "Carmine won't go near them fudge packers, thinks that shit'll rub off on him."

I held my tongue. Political correctness had not infected Big Tony's universe, and it probably never would.

I pushed the plate of cannelloni away from me and pushed my chair away from the table. I stood.

"That's your problem," I told the fat man. "I did my part."

I turned and stepped to the door.

Big Tony sputtered. "I didn't give you permission to leave."

"I didn't ask," I said. I opened the door, stepped through, and closed it behind me. I didn't hear whatever invectives Big Tony hurled at my back as I crossed the main dining room.

Carmine—Big Tony's remaining debt collector—was walking into the restaurant as I was walking out. We nodded to each other without speaking.

Austin did not know exactly how I earned my living, but he did know I owned a three-story French Second Empire home and that he had been quite happy overseeing the renovations and the redecorating since joining me in it two years earlier.

He was waiting for me in the living room when I returned home that night at a quarter past ten, wearing silk pajamas I'd given him the previous Christmas, reading the second book in a popular series of vampire novels, and nursing a glass of Chablis. He closed his book and placed it next to his wineglass on the end table. "How was your day?"

"Filled with meetings."

"And how did things go?" he asked as he stood.

"I was very persuasive," I said.

Austin's finger-length blond hair had been styled earlier that day, he was clean shaven, and he had not been long out of the shower because I could smell a lingering trace of his favorite body wash. He was exactly what I needed to see, and I felt my pulse quicken and my cock twitch. I look him in my arms and covered his soft lips with mine.

Our tongues met in a fiery dance of desire, and our kiss was long and deep and hard, and by the time it ended I had an erection straining against the inside of my boxers.

When the kiss ended, Austin said, "I made chicken and rice. You hungry?"

"Only for you." I pressed up against him and he noticed my turgid erection.

He slipped one hand between us, cupped my cock through the fabric of my slacks, and whispered hoarsely, "You've had a hard day."

Far harder than he could imagine. I had killed a man I had once fucked on a regular basis, and I had done it because that's what I did. I solved problems.

Austin pushed my jacket off my shoulders, and it slid down my arms. He caught it and laid it across the back of the couch. He unbuttoned my shirt and started pulling the tail from my waistband. As he reached around me, he found the holster at the small of my back and the .38 I carried in it. He made a face, and my cock began to wilt.

My belt was threaded through the holster. So, I unthreaded my belt from my belt loops, slipped the holster off, and placed it on the end table next to Austin's paperback and his wineglass.

"Why do you carry that nasty thing?"

"For protection."

He thought I managed investments for my two uncles, which was true as far as it went, and had no idea why I needed protection. We'd had this discussion before and there was only one way to end it: Remind Austin why he'd been removing my clothes. I slipped out of my shirt and then peeled off the wife beater beneath.

My live-in lover placed one palm on my hairy chest and purred softly. Then he drew one of my hands to his face and wrapped his lips around my middle finger. He sucked it into his mouth and my cock responded immediately.

The .38 apparently forgotten, Austin stripped off the rest of my clothes and then removed his silk pajamas, revealing his pale, nearly hairless body and precise manscaping.

He cupped my heavy nut sac in one hand and kneaded my nuts together while he wrapped the other hand around my cock and stroked his fist up and down a couple of times. Then he winked at me and said, "I'll meet you upstairs."

One of the first things we had done during renovation was convert the third floor into a master bedroom, creating a love nest in hardwood and indirect lighting, and we had spent many hours entwined in one another's arms once the renovation was complete.

I chased Austin up two flights of stairs, my attention

riveted on his smooth, white ass the entire way. We both knew I could have caught him without exerting any real effort, but it was a game we played. I finally caught him as we crossed the bedroom from the stairs and we tumbled across the king-size bed, wrestling one another until I had him pinned on the bed.

He lay flat on his back, his arms flung out to either side and held in place by my shins as I knelt above him. I was leaning forward, my hands flat against the wall above the headboard, and my nut sac dangled above his face.

Austin thrust out his tongue and tickled the hair on my nut sac. Then he lifted his head from the pillow and sucked my sac between his lips. He nipped at my nuts and rolled them around in his mouth, soaking my sac with his saliva.

My erect cock bobbed above Austin's face. I reached down and wrapped my fist around it. As he sucked my scrotum, I stroked myself. The faster I pumped my fist, the harder Austin sucked my nuts, and soon he was sucking so hard that pleasure mixed with pain.

I pumped harder and faster and soon couldn't stop myself. I came with a grunt and fired a thick stream of come across Austin's face and against the headboard. I leaned against the wall for a moment while my cock throbbed and oozed out another few drops of come.

Then I twisted off of Austin and flopped onto the bed beside him. He wiped his face with his hand, licked his fingers clean, and then bent over my crotch so that he could take my flaccid cock in his mouth and bring it back to life.

As soon as I was hard again, Austin rolled away from me, reached into the drawer of the nightstand on his side of the bed, and pulled out a tube of lube. He squeezed some onto his fingers and painted my erection with the slick stuff.

I took the tube from Austin and pushed him facedown on the bed. After squeezing a big glop of lube into the crack of his ass, I massaged it in. I slipped one finger into his tight sphincter and continued massaging until I could slip in a second.

"Quit teasing me," Austin whispered hoarsely, and I knew he was ready.

I positioned myself behind him, between his spread thighs, and grabbed his hips. I pulled his ass upward and knee-walked forward until I had the swollen head of my cock pressed against his slick ass hole. Then I thrust my hips forward and drove my cock deep inside my lover.

He moaned with pleasure and thrust his hips back to meet each of my powerful forward thrusts. I slammed into him again and again and again and soon the headboard was banging against the wall and the wall-mounted lamps above the bed were rattling, and I was grunting with exertion.

And then I came and came hard.

I fired a thick stream of come deep into Austin's ass, and I held his hips tight against my crotch until my cock finally quit throbbing and softened enough that I could pull away easily.

I flopped onto my back and Austin rolled over, into the cradle of my arm. After he fell asleep, I slipped out of bed and returned to the living room for my .38 and holster. I put them in the drawer of my nightstand and returned to bed, confident that I could reach the revolver should I need it for any reason.

I spent the next several weeks keeping tabs on Big Tony and his efforts to replace Little Stevie. No one in his organization understood The District and the men who populated it, and it appeared that Tony's heavy-handed tactics were causing one of his key revenue streams to dwindle to a trickle. It didn't help him any that I fomented resistance to his efforts by suggesting to his clients that a gay man could better serve their needs than Big Tony ever could.

The gentlemen I worked for had no idea I was undermining Tony and they increased their pressure on him to improve cash flow. Tony was old school, but he wasn't stupid, and he figured out what was happening before I was ready to make my move.

I came home one evening after spending a day in the District to find Big Tony sitting in Austin's spot on the couch, Carmine standing on the far side of the room, and Austin in a heap in the middle of the floor, a long cut on his right cheek and blood trickling from the corner of his mouth.

"He hit me," Austin said as soon as he saw me.

Big Tony had a small revolver nearly engulfed by his pudgy hand, and his hand rested in his lap. It was obvious that Tony had backhanded Austin and the revolver's sight had slashed Austin's cheek.

Carmine stood with his arms folded across his chest. He was accustomed to intimidating people with his size and with a face that looked like it had been hit repeatedly with the flat side of a shovel and the shovel was the worse for it, and I knew he would be slow to go for his gun if any shooting started. I returned my attention to Big Tony and the revolver in his fist.

He pointed it at me and accused, "You been going around behind my back."

I shrugged.

"You got chutzpah, boy, but you ain't too smart," he continued. He wasn't aiming the gun at me so much as he was talking with his hands. "Ain't nobody crosses me. Nobody."

"What's he talking about?" Austin asked from the floor.

I unbuttoned my jacket.

"We're gonna go for a little drive and settle this."

Big Tony started to heave himself off my couch. He was so big he needed both hands to leverage himself.

I had a brief moment of opportunity, and I took advantage of it. My hand darted behind my back and came out wrapped around my .38. I put a single shot through Big Tony's forehead, turned, and put two into Carmine's chest in the time it took him to unfold his arms.

Austin leapt to his feet and wrapped his arms around me.

I had two dead men in my living room and my live-in

boyfriend blubbering in my arms. The full impact of what I'd just done was sinking in, and I was getting a hard-on thinking about it. With Big Tony out of the way, there was an opportunity for someone to move up, and I was the obvious choice.

Exactly as I'd intended.

"Jesus," Austin muttered as one hand drifted from my back to my crotch. "You're turned on by this."

Apparently, he was, too. He unzipped my fly and unthreaded my turgid cock from my boxers. Then he dropped to his knees and took the head of my cock in my mouth. He wrapped one hand around my stiff shaft and pumped his fist up and down as he painted my cock head with his tongue. The zipper of my slacks pinched my cock skin as Austin jerked me off, a mixture of pleasure and pain that turned me on even more.

When he removed his hand from my cock and began to take a little more of my length into his mouth, I grabbed the back of his head and held it as I drove my cock deep into his oral cavity. Then I face-fucked him hard and fast, my zipper scratching his nose and cheeks.

He grabbed the backs of my thighs and held on until I couldn't restrain myself. I stiffened as I came, and I fired hot come against the back of his throat. He swallowed and swallowed again, and when my cock stopped throbbing, I pulled Austin to his feet and covered his mouth with mine. I tasted my come and the blood from his cut lip and I didn't care.

I needed to have a long conversation with Austin about how I earned my living and what part he would play in the future. After I called the cleaners, I started by telling Austin, "We'll need to redecorate."

WATCHING KYLE

I sat with my client, Christian Edwards III, and watched the big-screen screen television mounted on the wall of his den. I didn't immediately recognize either of the two men on the screen, but my client knew one of them. The pale young blond with the cock in his mouth was Christian's arm candy, and I was paying close attention to the other man because my client had given me a two-thousand-dollar retainer to find him.

The videographer had been careful not to capture the second man's face, but I saw just about everything else, from the dark hair on his ass to the way his erect cock tilted to the left. I also noticed the discolored pucker of skin on the left side of his chest where he'd once been shot with a small caliber bullet.

Kyle—the blond with the cock in his mouth— massaged the other man's heavy ball sac with one hand and fist-fucked his thick cock with the other. Before long, the other man's hips began pumping back and forth, and then the unidentified man grabbed the back of Kyle's head and drove his cock deep into Kyle's mouth. He drew back and drove forward maybe half a dozen times. Then his entire body stiffened, and Kyle's Adam's apple bobbed as he repeatedly swallowed what must have been a big load.

The camera operator slowly zoomed in on Kyle's mouth, and Kyle's lips nearly filled the screen as the other man pulled his deflating cock from Kyle's mouth. For a moment a thin thread of come connected Kyle's lips to the other man's cock. Then Kyle licked his lips, the come-thread broke, and the screen went blank.

My client had turned off the DVD player.

By then I had a throbbing erection. I glanced at my client—a fastidiously dressed, balding man near my age but packing more weight and less muscle—and decided against saying anything. I knew better than to mix business with pleasure.

Christian pushed himself off the black leather couch and ejected the DVD from the player. He turned and thrust it toward me.

I took the disk and asked, "Where did you get this?"

"I found it in Kyle's things, in this." Christian handed me a plain white disk mailer.

"Have you asked Kyle about it?"

"He doesn't know I have it," Christian explained, "and I don't want him to. I want to know who the other man is before I decide what to do about Kyle's infidelity."

I slipped the disk into the mailer and tucked both into a manila folder that contained a copy of the client contract I'd had Christian sign and a copy of the receipt I'd given him for the retainer. Then, confident that my cock had sufficiently deflated, I stood.

"There isn't much to work with," I told my client as he walked me to the door, not revealing that the discolored pucker of skin on the unidentified man's chest had reminded me of someone long forgotten.

Christian glanced at his wristwatch as we stepped onto the broad brick porch of his two-story colonial. "You'd best get started. Kyle is due home from the gym any minute now. It might be best if he didn't see you here."

Kyle Armstrong had the kind of body men like me lust after and men like my client pay to maintain. He spent several days a week at the gym, working with a personal trainer paid for by my client, and had a standing, weekly appointment at a chic salon where he had his hair styled, his body waxed, and his tan perfected. He wore designer-label clothing charged to my client's account and drove a new Lexus ISF leased under my client's name. In exchange all he had to do was keep his mouth shut, literally and figuratively, when he was in the company of other men.

Kyle had failed to do that. Worse, he had been caught giving lip service to an unidentified man for unknown reasons and had kept video evidence of his indiscretion.

Later that evening I sat on my couch, wearing nothing but hand lotion and a box of Kleenex, and watched the video until I had a cramp in my wrist and had learned everything I could. The two men were in the living room of someone whose taste ran to Rent-A-Center and Walmart, and sunlight streaming through an undraped bay window indicated a western-facing home in the late afternoon. The camera operator—who had briefly stepped between the window and the two men, momentarily casting a shadow across them—was a woman or a tranny. Razor burn on the back of Kyle's neck and the lack of hair anywhere on his body below that implied that he had visited the salon within hours of when the video was made. Because his standing appointment was for two o'clock Tuesdays, I felt certain the video had been made late on a Tuesday afternoon. A call to my client would help me determine which Tuesday Kyle had been late returning home from the salon.

I had a passing familiarity with video cameras. My earliest clients had been divorce lawyers seeking proof of infidelity to use against their clients' spouses, and I had hundreds of hours of video taken through keyholes, peepholes, and the half-closed blinds of women with women, women with men, and men with men, most of it on VHS cassettes stored in locked cabinets in the back room of my office. The videographer in this case had used a camera of much higher quality than a cell phone, something light enough to be hand-held, and the picture didn't shake and jerk and go in and out of focus the way an amateur's work usually did.

The bullet wound, though, is what kept my mind racing. That discolored pucker of skin on the left side of the unidentified man's chest reminded me of someone long forgotten, someone I should have called easily to mind but couldn't.

• • •

I slept fitfully, alternately dreaming about shoving my cock between Kyle's lips and about an encounter with a stranger sporting a bullet wound on the left side of his chest.

After I woke the next morning, I downed several cups of hot coffee and took a long, cold shower. Then I drove downtown, to the second-floor office of an alternative weekly, where I met with Karl Rumson, editor of the rag and a man I had known ever since he'd interviewed me for a piece on alternate careers for outed-and-no-longer-employed law enforcement officers. He wrote most of the paper himself, relying on unreliable and unpaid interns to fill the few column inches he couldn't fill each week using one of his many pseudonyms. As "Sir Stiffy," he reviewed man-on-man videos, rating them from one to five hard-ons, so I handed him the DVD of Kyle and we watched it on his laptop.

When the video ended, Rumson ejected the DVD and handed it to me.

"I know who the blond is," I told him. "I'm looking for the other guy. Have you seen him in anything?"

"You think he's a pro?"

"He looks familiar to me. I thought it might have been in one of those videos you gave me."

"I've seen a lot of cock," Rumson said, "but I've never seen that one before."

"Is there *anything* you can tell me about this?" I held up the DVD.

"The camerawork is familiar."

I perked up. "How so?"

He turned back to his laptop, opened a Web browser,

and clicked through to a listing on Craigslist.com advertising "Intimate Videography." He said, "She's the one made your video."

I read the four-word listing. "Intimate videography. Reasonable prices."

"How do I reach her?"

Rumson tapped the screen. The only contact information was a Craigslist.com reply-to address. "Send her a message. Tell her what you want. If she's interested, she'll contact you."

"This woman have a name?"

"None that I ever heard," he said. "And she only takes cash. In advance."

Rumson helped me fashion a brief message, and I included my cell phone number.

As I stood to leave, Rumson asked if I wanted any more videos to take home. "They're stacking up."

I had too many already, so I declined the offer.

Once I was back in my car, I phoned my client. He didn't answer.

Half an hour later I sat in my office and listened to my messages, returned two calls from prospective clients, and was about to watch Kyle do the unidentified guy again when my client called.

"It could have been any time," Christian said. "The Foundation Board meets the first Tuesday of every month, and the meetings often run late."

The videographer phoned a few minutes later, refused

to provide her name, and agreed to meet me at a coffee shop that afternoon to discuss the project I had proposed.

On my way to the coffee shop, I purchased a portable DVD player and stopped at an ATM to withdraw cash from my checking account.

I was sitting at a table outside, sipping a latte, when the videographer arrived and settled onto the seat across from me. She wore a red flannel shirt, worn jeans, and scuffed black hiking boots. Blond hair hung in waves to her shoulders, and she'd taken time with her makeup. I couldn't tell which way her pendulum swung, and I didn't ask.

I had the disk already in the DVD player, so I hit play and turned the screen toward her. "This your work?"

"It could have been better," she said. "I had to use natural light."

"Who hired you to shoot this?"

"I don't discuss my clients." She stood to go.

I reached out and grabbed her wrist. With my free hand I pulled a wad of twenties from my shirt pocket. "I just want a few minutes of your time," I said. "I'll make it worth your while."

She glared at me a moment and then sat back down. After I peeled a trio of twenties off the wad and placed them before her, she said, "The blond."

"Kyle Armstrong?"

"Kyle sounds right. I never heard his last name, and he always has a different man with him."

"This isn't the first time you've shot Kyle?"

She snorted. "He's one of my regulars. The first Tuesday of every month for more than two years."

"These men he's with," I said. "What are they like?"

"They're like you. Big. Ugly. Been around the block a few times too many." Nothing at all like his sugar daddy. "Sometimes they get rough with him. Why, you looking to hook up with him?"

"I'm looking for the other man in the video."

"Dirty Sanchez?"

"You know him?"

"Not well, and only by his screen name."

"He's a pro?"

"He thinks he is," she explained. "He's had bit parts in a few low-budget movies."

I knew then where I'd seen him—in a Roman orgy scene in one of the five-hard-on videos Rumson had given me several years earlier when one of my boyfriends dumped me. I'd watched that scene so many times my DVD had started to skip every time it came on.

I had one more question for the videographer. "How can I get copies of the other DVDs you made for Kyle?"

"I'll make duplicates and send them to you." She named a figure and I peeled off twenties until I reached it.

She scooped the twenties off the table, folded them in half, and slipped them into her shirt pocket. Then she walked away.

I drove home from the coffee shop and dug through my DVD collection until I found the title I needed. I shoved the DVD into my computer and fast-forwarded to the orgy scene. I worked back and forth until I was able to get a blurry screen capture that included Dirty Sanchez's face. Then I replaced that DVD with Kyle's DVD and did two screen captures—one a close-up of Sanchez's cock and the other an image that included the bullet wound in his chest. I printed all three screen captures on high gloss paper. Then I found the production company's local address on the back cover of the Roman orgy DVD case and headed out again.

The production company was in a warehouse sandwiched between an auto parts distributor and a printing company. The front office was little more than a waist-high counter with a metal desk behind it and two uncomfortable chairs and a plastic fern on the customer side. I slapped the bell on the counter and waited until a little guy who looked like he hadn't moisturized in decades stepped from the back.

He looked me up and down. "You here to read for *The Maltese Cockring?*"

"Excuse me?"

"We start shooting tomorrow. You here to read for the lead? You look like you could play Sam Splayed."

I told him I wasn't interested in a part in his next direct-to-DVD flick. I pulled the three screen captures from the folder in my hand and spread them across the counter. "I'm looking for this guy."

He glanced at the photos. "Dirty Sanchez?"

"What's his real name and where can I find him?"

"Don't know his real name, but he'll be here tomorrow. We're giving him a speaking role in this one."

"What time?"

"Noon. That's when we'll be shooting his part." He smiled and tapped the photo of Sanchez's erection. "And it's a pretty big part."

When I returned home, I found a small box waiting for me. Inside were several DVDs. I took them inside, fixed myself a drink, and then settled on the couch to watch them.

Each one featured Kyle, on his knees with a dick in his mouth or bent over some inanimate object taking a dick up his ass. After the third DVD I lost my objectivity. I'd left the hand lotion and Kleenex on the end table the previous evening, and I made use of it again when I started the fourth DVD.

The videographer was stationed in a bedroom, some place more upscale than the first video I'd seen. Kyle entered the picture wearing a blue turtleneck that hugged his torso like a second skin and khaki chinos with sharp creases. A large, jar-headed man with black hair gray at the temples and a face that looked like it had been smashed against a brick wall once too often followed close behind him. He wore dirty blue jeans and a blue work-shirt with Teddy emblazoned on an embroidered patch above his left breast.

As soon as they entered the bedroom, the big man grabbed Kyle's arm, spun him around, and pulled him close. He covered Kyle's mouth with his and shoved his tongue down Kyle's throat. The camera zoomed in on Kyle's face and I watched his eyelids fall to half-mast when the big man frenched him.

The camera slowly pulled back. Teddy had one arm wrapped around Kyle, the other buried in the front of Kyle's chinos. He pushed Kyle and away and unfastened his belt and his jeans. He pushed his jeans down from his hips. He wore no underwear, and his thick, erect phallus sprang into view.

Kyle dropped to his knees and took the head of Teddy's cock in his mouth. He wrapped one hand around the stiff shaft and began stroking forward and back, but Teddy would have none of that. He knocked Kyle's hand away, and then captured Kyle's head between his big hands and drove his cock down Kyle's throat until his balls slapped Kyle's chin.

He drew back and did it again.

And again.

The camera slowly zoomed in on the young blond's face until the entire screen was filled with the image of Teddy's cockshaft pistoning in and out of Kyle's mouth.

My cock had remained half-erect while I'd switched DVDs, but now it was fully engorged. I released it from my pants, squirted hand lotion into my palm and matched Teddy's rhythm.

He'd had a head start, so he came first. The camera had panned out just a bit so I could see Kyle's eyes widen in surprise as Teddy fired a load of come against the back of his throat. Then Kyle's Adam's apple bobbed up and down as he worked to swallow.

Teddy pulled his cock away and a last spasm fired a thin drop of come on Kyle's check, where it clung as Teddy pulled Kyle to his feet. The camera pulled back as the two men stripped and flung clothes on the floor in their haste.

As always, Kyle was tanned and denuded. His partner in the video was anything but, with dark hair covering much of his body, and the skin beneath hadn't seen the sun in quite some time. He was thick and muscular, though, and his fat phallus was quickly regaining its former stature.

He spun Kyle around and bent him over the bed, then grabbed a half-used tube of lube and slathered it over his fingers. He covered his cock with it first and then fingered a glob of it into Kyle's ass crack.

The camera zoomed in on Teddy's hand and I watched as he massaged Kyle's tight pucker. He eased one thick finger into the blond and a moment later it was joined by a second.

I couldn't restrain myself any longer and quickly grabbed a tissue to catch the thick glob of come that spewed from my cock. As I relaxed and leaned back on my couch, spent from my handshake with the Pope, Teddy replaced his fingers with his cock, easing the fat head into Kyle.

The camera drew back, again returning to a two-shot. Teddy grabbed Kyle's hips and slammed his cock all the way into the younger man. Then he drew back and did it again. And again.

The camera angle was wrong, but it seemed that Kyle's cock was also erect because he reached between his legs. I watched his arm pumping while the bigger man behind him was slamming into his ass again and again and again.

My own cock twitched as if it wanted another go-round with Father Thumb and his four sons, but the two men on screen came before that could happen.

Teddy slammed into Kyle one last time and practically roared as his orgasm exploded. Kyle came just a moment later and I saw a thick stream of come fire from beneath him.

After they both collapsed on the bed, I fast-forwarded the DVD. There wasn't anything else of interest.

I watched the rest of the DVDs, taking my cock in my hand twice more before I finished watching all of them, and then I wondered what I had learned.

As the videographer had told me, Kyle had a thing for big, ugly guys like me. And he liked to capture his encounters on tape.

I went to sleep that night with that thought gnawing at the back of my brain. It was still gnawing at me when I returned to the video production company the next day to find Dirty Sanchez.

The little guy I'd spoken to the day before pointed him out, though I would have found Sanchez on my own if I'd been close enough to him to see the puckered bullet wound in his chest.

He sat naked on a canvas chair, a beer in one hand and a cigarette in the other. His thick phallus, longer flaccid than mine was fully erect, lay on the chair between his widespread thighs.

Sanchez glanced at me as I settled onto the chair next to his. Then he took a long drag on his cigarette.

I flipped a photo print of Kyle Armstrong into his line of sight. "You know this kid?"

When Sanchez glanced at the picture, I caught a glimmer of recognition in the way his cock twitched. He said, "Who wants to know?"

I flipped my P.I. badge under his nose, too fast for him examine it closely.

"So, what'd the kid do?"

"It's not what the kid did that interests me," I said. "It's who did the kid."

Sanchez sucked down the last of his cigarette and dropped the butt into his beer can where it died with a hiss. "You know I did, or you wouldn't be here."

"Why him?"

"Why not?" Sanchez said. "He's a beautiful boy. I would have fucked him even if he hadn't paid."

"He paid you?"

"Screen test. He presented himself as a producer, but I knew better. I been around enough to tell who's legit and who ain't. He's a poseur with money that knows a dyke with a camera. He wanted it hard, fast, and rough. So, I gave it to him, pocketed the dough, and ain't looked back."

Someone behind us called out, "Be ready in five."

"I got to get back to work," Sanchez said as he took his cock in his hand and began massaging it back to life. "They're too cheap to hire fluffers."

"One last question."

His cock was half erect by then, rising like a sleeping giant.

"The hole in your chest. Where'd you get it?"

"Jealous sugar daddy caught me with his squeeze."

I didn't tell Sanchez that he might have another sugar daddy after him and instead left him to his work.

I had burned through most of my client's retainer by then, so I made an appointment to meet him later that evening, to update him and see if he wanted me to burn through a few thousand more of his dollars.

We met at his house, and he led my back to the den with the big-screen television. I had all of the DVDs with me, and I handed them to him after we settled into our seats.

"There are twenty-five encounters recorded on these," I said, "including the one you've already seen. The videographer says she shoots one the first Tuesday of every month, and Kyle's never with the same man twice. I've watched them all and can confirm that there are no duplicates."

"You've watched all of these?" He held up the DVDs.

"I fast-forwarded through the boring parts."

My client seemed aghast. "So, you've watched Kyle

cheat on me twenty-five times? Did you get your rocks off?"

I didn't admit a thing. "It was part of the job you hired me to do," I explained. "Maybe more than you hired me to do. You just wanted me to find one guy, not identify twenty-four more."

"And did you find him?"

I told him about Dirty Sanchez, I told him that Kyle pretended to be a producer, and I told him that Kyle paid the men in the videos.

"So that's supposed to make me feel better?"

"You didn't hire me to be your therapist," I said.

I heard someone enter the room behind us, and I turned to see Kyle standing in the open doorway. He looked even more beautiful in person than he did on screen.

My client saw him, too. Christian pushed himself to his feet and threw the stack of DVDs at his young lover. "You little tramp!"

Kyle smiled and it was quite a charming smile, with just enough twinkle in his eye. "Excuse me?"

"These...these...these...videos of you with other men." My client stormed across the room. "How dare you go behind my back and—"

"But I did it for you," Kyle said.

That stopped my client.

"You know you don't like it rough."

"I—"

"And I was just trying to protect you from that scene."

"But you taped your encounters."

"To protect myself. You never know what men like that will say."

That was my cue to leave. I stood and let myself out of the house without another word to either of them. The last thing I wanted to do was watch Kyle smooth-talk himself into getting my client to apologize, and I had the feeling that was about to happen.

Maybe I was wrong, though. Maybe my client was less of a cream puff than I suspected. Maybe Kyle wasn't able to talk himself out of his jam.

Several weeks later Kyle's body—sans genitalia—was pulled from the river. That same day a large envelope containing $10,000 in small bills arrived at my office with a note from Edward Christian III thanking me for services rendered.

I never told the IRS about the extra income, and Kyle's murder remains unsolved.

Kyle's hard to forget, though. Before I gave my client the DVDs, I made duplicates and stored them with the videotapes I'd made earlier in my career. Maybe someday, when I'm alone, and horny, and able to forget what happened to Kyle, I'll watch them again.

He was such a beautiful boy.

If only he'd kept his mouth shut.

HOUSE OF SEVEN INCHES

The real estate listing said "fixer-upper" but the two-story house looked more like a "burner-downer." It had been empty for years and was located just south of the middle of nowhere, but I bought it anyway.

My first call was to a plumber, intending to follow it with calls to an electrician and a roofer after I received the plumber's estimate. The plumber and I were standing in the kitchen when he said, "The last owner was one of your kind."

I turned and glared at the weathered old man. He was my grandfather's age and smelled of cheap tobacco and cheaper beer. "And what kind is that?"

He held up one arm and let his wrist go limp. "You know."

"And what happened to him?"

"He—" The plumber stopped and looked like he was searching for the right word. Finally, he said, "disappeared."

"You mean he moved away?"

The old man shrugged. "One day he was here. The

next day he wasn't. After he missed a couple of payments and his phone was disconnected, the bank sent a man out to look the place over. A couple of months after that the bank repossessed and put the contents of the house up for auction. I got the missus a real nice set of china."

"He just walked away?"

"Your guess is as good as any," the plumber said. "Sheriff Johnson looked the place over, said there were no signs of foul play, but the previous owner ain't turned up and he ain't come back."

I looked around, not certain what I expected to see that was any different than what I'd already seen. The kitchen was in no better shape than the rest of the house, and it needed serious renovation before I would ever feel comfortable.

The plumber patted the front pocket of his blue work shirt where he'd put the notebook he'd used while I'd explained all the work I wanted done, and said, "I'll do some figuring tonight and drop my estimate by tomorrow."

I walked him to the front door and stood on the porch watching his pickup until it disappeared around a curve in the road. Then I returned to the kitchen and used half a can of air freshener to eliminate the plumber's lingering scent.

For the next several months I had men in and out of my house, some of them quite attractive but none of them approachable. They replaced the roof and the windows, rewired and replumbed where necessary, and remodeled the kitchen and both bathrooms to my specifications. I replastered the walls and refinished the hardwood floors myself. Soon there was nothing left to do but paint, furnish, and decorate, all things I could do on my own, and I soon realized just how isolated my new house was.

I had sold my condo in the city shortly before the housing market cratered, and I was among the first wave of employees to accept my employer's buyout offer, getting out while the getting was good. Most of my money was invested in things that weren't badly hurt by the stock market plunge, so I could survive comfortably for several years without additional income. I had hoped to return to my first love—writing—and thought I needed solitude to write the novel that had been nagging at me for several years. What I most assuredly did not need was the drama Kyle brought into my life, so I had left him behind when I moved, certain that he would quickly become someone else's drama queen.

Even so, it was difficult to forget Kyle completely. When he wasn't talking, he had the sweetest mouth I'd ever stuck my dick into. I was thinking about that one evening in the shower, after a long day spent painting. The warm water relaxed me, I had a handful of liquid soap, an erection I could have used to pound nails, and I hadn't been with a man since moving to the country several months earlier.

I knew what I had to do, and I did it. I closed my eyes and took my cock in my hand, remembering the last time Kyle had been on his knees in front of me. We'd spent the evening at Throttlebottom's, a dark little bar where most of our friends hung out, and we'd returned to my apartment a little more toasted than usual. As soon as I pushed the door closed, I pushed Kyle back against it. I covered his lips with mine and then drove my tongue into his mouth. He sucked on it and sucked hard. He was just as horny as me and we stripped off our clothes, tossing them aside until we were both naked.

With my hands on his softly rounded shoulders, I encouraged Kyle to his knees. He kissed his way down my chest to my belly button, found my treasure trail, and followed it to my neatly sculpted nest of black hair. He cupped my balls in one hand and wrapped the other around my cock shaft. Then he took my swollen purple cock head in his mouth and painted it with his tongue.

He was taking too long, so I grabbed the back of his head and thrust my hips forward, sinking my cock into Kyle's mouth until I could feel his warm, boozy breath tickle my crotch hair. Then I pulled back and thrust forward again.

My hips began moving with the memory, fucking my fist as I remembered fucking Kyle's face. Faster and faster, unable to restrain myself.

Then my breath caught, my entire body stiffened for the briefest of moments, and I spewed come all over the shower wall. Unable to catch my breath immediately, I leaned against the newly installed tile and let the warm water cascade over my body until I could finish bathing.

When I stepped out of the shower a few minutes later I caught the unmistakable scent of Old Spice, reminding me first of my stepfather and then of my scout master, neither of whom had understood me but both of whom had encouraged me not to hide behind a societally imposed facade. I smiled.

Then I realized someone had been watching me shower. I wrapped a towel around my waist and called out, "Who's there?"

When I received no response, I hurried through the house, checking every room for evidence that someone was in the house with me. There weren't many places to hide—I'd finished painting but had not yet furnished most of the rooms. I looked under my bed, opened all the closets, and even looked inside the dryer. I also checked every door and every window and found them all locked from the inside.

Although I was still bothered by the feeling that I'd been watched, I returned to the bathroom to finish pampering myself. By then the scent of Old Spice had disappeared, replaced by the floral scent of my body wash and the barely perceptible odor of my own come. I shaved, I tweezed, and I moisturized, not letting my personal grooming falter despite my dating drought.

Then I tucked myself into bed with a thick paperback and read until I was too tired to keep my eyes open. I fell asleep with the hall light on, just in case.

By the time my living room furniture was delivered two weeks later, I'd forgotten about the creepy feeling I'd had that night. With more furniture in the house, it felt more like a home, and I felt more comfortable in it. At that point I still lacked furniture for the office, so I had half a sheet of plywood resting on two sawhorses to hold my laptop computer and my printer, and I sat on a three-step aluminum stepladder. The novel was going nowhere—I'd written the first page a dozen times—but I wasn't deterred. I knew I would start my real work once I finished work on the house.

Late one afternoon I sat at my makeshift desk, a number two pencil in my hand and a yellow legal pad in front of me, stared out the window at the backyard, a vast tract of untended grass and overgrown shrubs that desperately needed my attention, and pondered the umpteenth rewrite of my first page. My mind drifted, first to the job I'd left behind in the city and then to Kyle. It had been months since I been with another man and several days since I'd handled the problem myself.

As I thought about Kyle—about his golden, shoulder-length hair, his pale blue eyes, and his full lips—my cock began to react, causing my pants to tighten at my crotch. I adjusted myself with my free hand.

I was surprised when I caught a whiff of Old Spice and felt a moist pair of lips on the nape of my neck. I spun around quickly, knocking my legal pad to the floor.

There was no one behind me. I was alone in my office.

After I retrieved my legal pad and returned it to my makeshift desk, I wiped my fingers against my neck. They came away damp. I considered my fingertips for a moment before convincing myself that I had been sweating and that what I had actually felt was a trickle of sweat rolling down my neck. My daydreaming about Kyle had made me imagine something else.

I pushed myself away from my desk and left my office. I knew I was alone, but I checked every room just in case. I found no one else in the house and nothing out of place. I grabbed a beer from the fridge and stepped out on the back porch to drink it. My backyard looked even worse from downstairs than it did from my second-floor office, and I knew I would need to tend to it soon.

I drove into town two days later and made my first stop the town's only hardware store. I selected a variety of tools to help me deal with the overgrown yard and was staring at a display of hoes when I heard a voice behind me.

"You the one that bought the Samuels' place?"

I turned to find a weathered old man leaning on an aluminum walker. He made my plumber look like a youngster.

"Yeah," I said. "I am."

"Heard you been fixing up the place."

"I'm doing what I can."

"Don't get too attached." He coughed into his fist.

"Why's that?"

"You won't be there long," he said.

I looked a question at him.

"Your kind don't stay around here."

"My kind?"

"City folk." He coughed into his fist again. "You and

your city ways. You all want something you can't find around here."

"I'll be fine."

"That's what the last guy said," the man said, "but he didn't last long."

The old man glared at me, and I glared back. He blinked first and then shuffled away without further comment.

I took my selections to the front counter where an acne-scarred teenager rang up my charges. After I paid him, he said, "Sheriff Johnson bothering you?"

I glanced toward the rear of the store, but the weathered old man and his aluminum walker were out of sight. "That was the sheriff?"

"He used to be, years ago," the kid said. "My dad says that back in the day Johnson ran the town with an iron fist. He still thinks he does, but most people ignore him."

I attacked the front yard first, collapsing into bed each evening with sore muscles and a sense of satisfaction. Nearly two weeks after my conversation with Sheriff Johnson, after I had finished with the front yard and planned to begin work on the back, I caught a glimpse of myself in the full-length mirror mounted on the back of my bedroom door. I was in the process of stripping off my clothes and I stopped to examine myself. All the hard work on the house and the yard had changed me.

Where once I had been soft in the middle, with no noticeable muscle definition, I had developed the kind of body I had once admired on others, and I was especially pleased that I sported a taut abdomen with clear signs of a developing six-pack. Hard physical labor had done for my body what years of gym membership had not. Kyle would be surprised by the change, as would my other friends, but I had no desire to return to the city, even to gloat.

After I shoved my dirty clothes in the hamper, I showered, pampered myself, and crawled into bed. I no longer slept with the hall light on, and the room was nearly back. The little bit of moonlight that usually filtered in through a gap in the drapes was hidden behind storm clouds that had been threatening to break loose all evening.

I was almost asleep when I felt weight on the bed behind me and caught the scent of Old Spice. My eyes snapped open. I knew there would be no one in bed with me if I rolled over, just like I knew there was no one else in the house. I wasn't about to climb out of bed and tromp through all the rooms to prove it. I closed my eyes.

The weight shifted and I opened my eyes again. I felt a hand on my left hip under the covers and still I didn't roll over. The weight shifted again, and I felt someone press against my back. Warm lips brushed my neck. A thick erection that must have been seven inches long nestled in the crack of my ass. The hand on my hip slid down to my crotch and cupped my balls. My cock began to swell.

Nearly a year had passed since I'd been with another man and occasionally taking matters in my own hands had done nothing to relieve my sexual frustration. I squeezed my eyes shut and convinced myself that I was having a particularly tactile dream.

The hand cupping my balls moved to my cock and I felt thick fingers make a fist around my rapidly stiffening shaft. The fist gripped my cock firmly and then moved up my shaft, stopping when the encircling thumb and forefinger reached my spongy soft helmet head. Then it moved down until the heel of the hand pressed against my pubic bone. The fist continued moving up and down, slowly at first and then with increasing speed.

As I was being fist-fucked, I felt a pair of lips travel around the back of my neck, gently at first, and then with increasing urgency. More than once I felt teeth nip at my neck. My breath began to come in little gasps as my orgasm drew closer and closer. Then, unable to restrain myself, I caught my breath and held it as I fired warm spunk all over my sheets.

Before I could catch my breath, the weight sifted behind me, and the hand holding my spasming cock released its grip. The hand moved between my thighs and encouraged me to lift my left leg. When I did, I felt the cock nestled between my butt cheeks slide down until the cock head pressed against the tight sphincter of my ass. My entire body was relaxed following my orgasm, and the cock head slipped into me with minimal resistance. Then, with one powerful thrust, the entire cock was buried deep within me.

Hips pulled back and pushed forward, the unseen cock driving into me hard and fast, and I pushed backward to accept every powerful thrust. Kyle had never fucked me like this, had never taken me in the middle of the night and had his way with me, and I moaned with unrestrained pleasure.

Lightning flashed outside, illuminating the entire bedroom through a thin crack in the drapes. For a split second I saw my reflection in the mirror mounted on the back of the bedroom door and I saw the covers bunched up as if two people were in the bed.

And then, with one last powerful thrust that buried the unseen cock deeper inside me than ever before, the cock stopped moving. I thought I heard a man moan with pleasure, and I felt a rush of warm air against my ear. But, at that same moment, thunder rolled across the night sky, completely obliterating any other sounds I might have thought I heard.

Then the storm clouds opened, and rain pelted the house. I felt asleep listening to the rain, convinced that someone was spooning me from behind, yet knowing full well that the only thing behind me was my imagination.

A few days later I discovered an old well on the property. It was little more than a hole in the ground, the low rock wall encircling the hole mostly collapsed, the boards covering the hole rotted away, and the entire thing covered by overgrown brush. I was tromping through the brush and would have fallen into the well if something hadn't stopped me at the last moment, something that felt like a hand pressing against my chest.

I didn't know who else to call, so I called the plumber and told him what had happened.

"You found the well, did you?"

"You knew about it?"

"Every house that old had its own well. Most of them are sealed to prevent accidents."

"Do you know someone who can take care of it for me?"

"I'll send my nephew over tomorrow," my plumber said. "He's a licensed contractor. You'll like him."

The plumber's nephew, a wiry man a few years younger than me, arrived early the next morning. My hair was still damp from the shower, and I was nursing my first mug of coffee as we walked out to the well.

He aimed the beam of his flashlight into the hole and rubbed his chin. "Before we can seal the well," he explained as he looked me over in an overtly sexual way, a way that no other man had since I'd moved into the house, "we have to clear out the debris that's fallen into it. I can call a couple of guys and get started on the job this morning."

We haggled over price for a few minutes before I gave him the go-ahead. He snapped open his cell phone as I headed into the house. I was hanging curtains in the dining room and didn't think anything about what was happening in my backyard until my plumber's nephew pounded on my back door.

"We got a problem," he said when I joined him on the

back porch. He touched my forearm with the tips of his fingers. "There's a body down the well."

My backyard became a crime scene and was soon overrun with sheriff's deputies and nosey townsfolk. The elected coroner wasn't a medical doctor—he was a funeral home director—so the remains were sent to Dallas for examination.

The remains were quickly identified as Nick Samuels—the house's previous owner—and Samuels was given a proper burial after an autopsy determined the cause of death. Samuels had been shot once in the back of the head and his body thrown in the well.

There's no statute of limitations for murder, so the new sheriff arrested the old sheriff and his aged cronies. In their day a jury of their peers might not have convicted the three men, but times had changed, and more than half of the jury consisted of the type of people Sheriff Johnson and his cronies had worked to keep out of the county. The trial lasted a week and the jury deliberated less than an hour.

My testimony was minimal, confirming that I owned the property and that I had discovered the well where the body was found. They never asked and I never mentioned the presence in my house all those months when I was renovating it.

Six months after the trial ended, after I had put the finishing touches on the house, I visited the cemetery and stood beside the previous owner's gave. As I told Samuels everything I had done to the house, I felt someone take my hand and I caught a hint of Old Spice wafting past me. I didn't glance to the side but kept my attention riveted on the headstone until I finished my tale.

As I finished, the hand holding mine squeezed tightly for a moment and then disappeared.

I returned home, grabbed a legal pad and a pencil and sat on the back porch.

I was finally alone in my house.

Maybe it was time to start the novel. Maybe it was time to call the plumber's nephew and find out if I had correctly interpreted his intentions.

ABOUT THE AUTHOR

Michael Bracken is the author of several books, but is better known as the author of more than 1,200 short stories, including erotica published in the Lambda Award-nominated anthologies *Show-offs* and *Team Players* and in *Best Gay Erotica 2013, Best New Erotica 4, Fifty Shades of Grey Fedora, Fifty Shades of Green, Flesh & Blood: Guilty as Sin, Gent, Hot Blood: Strange Bedfellows, Oui, Ultimate Gay Erotica 2006*, and many other anthologies and periodicals. Learn more at www.CrimeFictionWriter.com.

PUBLISHING ACKNOWLEDGEMENTS

"Mutable Memories," *Men of the Manor*, Cleis Press, 2014

"The Gimp, the Vig, and the Ring," *Muscle Men*, Cleis Press, 2010

"The Gunsel, the Nance, and the Redheaded Rooster," *Mob Men on the Make*, StarBooks Press, 2011

"What a Rush," *Pledges*, Cleis Press, 2013

"The Hitter and the Stall," *Wild Boys*, Cleis Press, 2012

"Stand By Your Man," *When a Man Loves a Man*, Xcite, 2011

"Mac and Cheese Get Boxed," *Kept Against His Will II*, StarBooks Press, 2012

"Tides," *Beautiful Boys*, Cleis Press, 2010

"Smooth Strokes," *Boys Getting Ahead*, StarBooks Press, 2010

"Meat and Potatoes," *Biker Boys*, Cleis Press, 2010

"Run for the Border," *Homeboys*, Cleis Press, 2015

"Queer Bait," *Freshmen*, June 2009

"Lipstick in the Rain," *Under the Desert Sky*, Xcite, 2011

"In the Closet," *Show-Offs*, Cleis Press, 2013

"Dicked," *Nasty Boys*, Cleis Press, 2013

"Do the Hustle." Original to this volume.

"Reprieve," *I Like to Watch*, Cleis Press, 2010

"Making Room at the Top," *Homo Thugs*, StarBooks Press, 2010

"Watching Kyle," *Video Boys*, StarBooks Press, 2010

"House of Seven Inches," *The Call of the Night*, Xcite, 2011

ALSO FROM MICHAEL BRACKEN

All-American Male
Men in Love and Lust #1

When college student Bernie is dragged to a Christmas party where he knows nobody, the last thing he expects is to be naked and between the thighs of the sexiest man he's ever met.

While older men aren't usually his thing, there's something about Professor Maeyer that gets Bernie going in ways he hasn't felt for a long time. So, when the party ends and everyone's gone home and it's just Bernie and Professor Maeyer, he gets a deeper education, the kind that can't be taught in class, the kind that can only be taught in the bedroom.

Bernie's about to learn just how much Professor Maeyer can blow his mind (and his load).

"Learning Curve" is just one of nineteen scorching hot and smutty-as-hell stories in this sweaty, throbbing, pounding collection of gay erotica from Michael Bracken, acclaimed author of erotic short fiction.

Available now in ebook and paperback

ALSO FROM MICHAEL BRACKEN

Sporting Wood
Men in Love and Lust #3

High-rise window washer Joe is used to seeing things on the job that he really shouldn't, but he's gotten good at ignoring the sights. That is, until his latest gig of washing the windows of a condominium has him like a peeping-tom watching two hot-as-hell men go at it in the supposed privacy of their bedroom.

When he's spotted by the men, he fears the worst—and he can't lose this job. But instead of calling the cops, one of the men holds a business card up to the window, giving Joe his name and number.

After struggling with whether or not to call the man—and realizing he's thought of nothing else since—Joe dives in crotch-first, leading him into a whole new world of sexual adventures.

"High-Rise Hook-Up" is just one of nineteen scorching hot and smutty-as-hell stories in this sweaty, throbbing, pounding collection of gay erotica from Michael Bracken, acclaimed author of erotic short fiction.

Publishes October 27, 2023, in ebook and paperback

www.ingramcontent.com/pod-product-compliance
Lightning Source LLC
Chambersburg PA
CBHW022011010726
47494CB00003B/994